'I didn't want to leave Cornwall. What about all my friends? And sailing? Last summer had been so fantastic. The winter ahead looked dull and bleak.

'But it wasn't like that at all. I think I grew up a bit during that winter and although I felt miserable at times I was hardly lonely!

'And I did make new friends.
There was Celia.
And Mike – well, it wasn't exactly love at first sight . . .
As for Charles – I never thought I'd meet a real, live star!
But then, I didn't think I'd ever fly. Or go into business.

'But best of all was seeing dreams come true . . .'

This is the second book about Fran Tremayne, the funny and irrepressible heroine of *Wheelchair Summer*. (She's now grown out of her Cornish nickname, Daffy.) *Winter Song* tells the story of the following winter. In her own determined way, Fran believes in miracles. And sees them happen.

WINTER SONG

Dorothy Oxley

A LION PAPERBACK

Copyright © 1983 Dorothy Oxley

Published by
Lion Publishing
Icknield Way, Tring, Herts, England
ISBN 0 85648 542 X
Albatross Books
PO Box 320, Sutherland, NSW 2232, Australia
ISBN 0 86760 435 2

First edition 1983

Cover photograph: Lion Publishing/Jon Willcocks

Printed and bound in Great Britain by
Collins, Glasgow

Contents

CHAPTER 1

CRYING FOR THE CREEK

I didn't cry until we'd left Peveran. I waved to my friends and then just sat stiff and frozen, looking straight ahead. I couldn't bear to turn and see the creek with the sun shining on it and think that if I ever got to sail on it again, it would only be as a Holiday Person. An emmet! That's what we called them in Cornwall. I tried to forget our little house that looked across to a copse where badgers lived. It now belonged to Mr Grayling, who'd been after it for years. I didn't even *like* Mr Grayling!

The cats had gone ahead with Dad and the furniture, in a lorry. There were just Mum and me and a heap of suitcases in our old banger. My Mirror dinghy was with Serena. I'd have been happy to give it to her (after all, she'd been my best friend since we were both knee-high to a bee) but her dad insisted on buying it. So I ended up accepting seventy pounds, though he said it was worth a lot more. I didn't want more. I just wanted it to be happy and boats aren't happy unless they're sailed. Where I was going was right inland, with just a measly river and no sailing club within about fifteen miles! And I hadn't even sailed my Mirror. It had been a present from the father of a boy whose life I'd saved that summer, but I'd hurt my back saving him. By the time I was allowed to do energetic things again it was October and I didn't have a wetsuit.

'Your Grandad's place is next to a flying club,' Mum said, weaving her way round Survival-of-the-Fittest roundabout. 'Perhaps you might get a chance to go up in a plane.'

Another time, I would have jumped at the idea — but not now. I still couldn't speak. We were on the Truro bypass, near enough to see Dad's shop. There'd been no problem in selling the lease of that, but I bet it had broken his heart as much as leaving Peveran was breaking mine. Why, oh why, had that drunken driver crashed into Grandad's car?

Then I gave up trying to be brave and bawled my eyes out. So what if I was old enough not to cry? Everything I loved best in life had been snatched away from me! Well, not *everything* (I know I over-dramatize a bit sometimes, I think I may end up being an actress as well as a writer). But I had lost my friends, my school, my sailing, my lovely Cornish home. How could life ever be the same again? Worst of all, was having to say goodbye to Andy. I suppose I couldn't have really called him my *boyfriend*, but he was special and our friendship had seemed so right that I'd felt sure it would go on for ever and one day turn into love and we'd get married. Sometimes I'd even practised writing my married name in my school notebooks — Fran MacKay. But now I might never have a chance of being Mrs MacKay because I was going three hundred miles away, and worse, there was a girl called Tamsin in Andy's form who had always fancied him and would be just waiting to get her claws into him the minute I was gone! So do you blame me for sitting in the passenger seat, howling?

Mum let me cry. When I'd subsided a bit, she said gently, 'At least we'll still be living in the countryside. And there's a girl of about your own age living at the airfield opposite, who also goes to the convent school. It's marvellous we've been able to get you in there, and on a scholarship too.'

Marvellous? A *convent*, after my lovely, free and easy school in Truro? She had to be kidding! The only good thing would be walking to school each day along the river bank, instead of catching a bus. And what if I didn't like the girl opposite, or she didn't like me? We'd met briefly when I'd come down for holidays − Celia or something her name was − but she hadn't made much of an impression.

I blew my nose and studied my red, blotchy face in the driving mirror as Mum muttered something rather rude about a man who passed us just before the narrow bridge in Tresillian, forcing her to brake sharply.

'There won't be an Andy, or a Serena, or a Jane, or a John,' I wailed.

'You'll soon make new friends. Anyway, someone had to help your Grandad out, and we were the only ones who could move comparatively easily and quickly.'

'You mean none of our relatives would give up their careers and lifestyles, but we're soft,' I grunted rebelliously.

'Would you rather we'd left it so that Grandad died of worry because he knew the Nurseries would have to be sold? He'll never be able to manage on his own again.'

Put like that, it made me feel pretty mean. 'Of course not!' I protested. 'But I reckon I deserve a bit of a moan! I'm fed up with being stiff-upper-lip! Why did it have to happen? It's not *fair*!'

'I didn't really want to leave Peveran, either,' Mum admitted.

'But you're naturally unselfish − I'm not!'

She gave me a rueful, sideways sort of smile but didn't say anything. I was quiet, too, thinking how Andy and Serena (Podge that was, but she'd slimmed) had both asked me back for holidays, but I knew it wouldn't be the same. They'd have got new friends and our lives would be too different for the old closeness to happen again.

9

'You could buy a canoe with your Mirror money. The river comes up to the lawn, remember?'

I remembered, all right! On holiday visits I'd splashed about in that river – it was really just an overgrown, weedy stream. Still, I supposed I could clean it out and swim in it. And it could be quite fun, watching the little planes take off and land at the airfield opposite. Maybe, as Mum said, I could even scrounge a flight one day – I'd never flown, it's the sort of luxury my family can't afford.

'I don't know much about gardening!' was my last feeble wail.

'The lad who's been running things since the accident does,' Mum said. He's Steve Harris – remember him? He's been working for your Grandad ever since he left school. There's a student who's working at the Nurseries in his vacation, too – Paul Kearton. He lives in. He worked there in the summer as well, so he knows what to do. But they can't manage the business side of things, and the idea is that your Dad takes over the office and does some work in the garden, while you and I help where we can. We'll soon learn!'

'And when Grandad's better, will we have to find a new home and shop?'

'No,' Mum said softly. 'This is a permanent thing, Fran. Everything's happened so quickly we've not had time to explain properly, but the fact is that your Grandad will probably be a semi-invalid for the rest of his life.'

'Oh, I didn't realize things were that bad!' I muttered, horrified. Poor old Grandad! He'd always been a tough, active old bird, and he'd hate it if he had to be dependent on anybody.

After that, of course, I had to stop moaning. Not because I felt more cheerful, but what had I really got to complain about, compared to Grandad? So I quit crying and started navigating, trying to make myself believe I wanted nothing

10

more than a home next to a weedy river and an airfield, a convent school and a host of unknown but sure to be marvellous new friends. As an added bonus, I told myself I'd at least be able to drop my Peveran nickname of Daffy, which I thought I'd outgrown, and be Fran Tremayne of Tremayne's Nurseries, Stoke Denman, Buckinghamshire.

But I had to admit, 262 miles later, that I still hadn't quite convinced myself I was happy!

As we got further East, we ran into snow. After all, it was December. Thinking of Christmas without my friends I almost cried again, but stopped myself by thinking of Grandad having to spend Christmas in hospital, which had to be far worse.

Anyway, the snow was pretty well cleared on the roads, and it improved my first view of my new home. Although I'd been there before, it had always been in summer. At Christmas, Grandad had come down to us, or we'd all gone to see one of my uncles. The last time I'd seen Tremayne's Nurseries, there'd been masses of flowers everywhere; now it was all Christmas trees, quiet, snow-dusted earth and pot plants in the greenhouses. Fir trees surrounded the house and office, the shop and stable block – everything coated with snow like a Christmas card.

'We're keeping the house aired for Grandad, of course,' Mum explained. 'And Paul has a bedsit there. But we're actually going to live in the converted stable block. It's a bit primitive and not quite finished – your Grandad put work in hand before his accident, planning to let it – but it is warm.'

'Where does Steve live?'

'Oh, with his family in the village – his Mum runs the Post Office. And Paul, of course, goes back to a student hostel in London during term time.'

Mum parked the car, and smiled in the direction of a

boy, about seventeen or eighteen, who was flogging a Christmas tree to a woman in a Land Rover. I remembered him dimly – enough to know he was Steve, a tall boy with a kind, friendly face.

'The boys have been doing their own meals since Grandad's accident,' Mum said, 'but I gather they're no experts and will be glad to eat with us.'

I smiled and waved at Steve, who waved back; then I helped Mum unload the car. Our furniture had arrived and had been put inside, but the lorry driver and his mate, friends of Dad's, were staying the night. As I staggered into the kitchen of our new home, carrying two cases, I saw them sitting in front of a woodburning stove. It looked homely, somehow.

'Your Dad's gone to visit your Grandad,' one of the men told me, pouring two more cups of coffee for Mum and me. 'We put the cats up in your room – they're not very happy.'

'Poor loves!' I wanted to go up and comfort the cats, but Mum asked me to take coffee and cake to Steve and Paul first. Apparently Mrs Burnett, the lady from the airfield opposite, had come over and brought a snack lunch for Dad and the removal men, plus a cake, as a sort of welcome present for us. Nice, eh? It was a chocolate cake, too!

I found Steve in the office, with a gas heater going full blast. He was glad to see the coffee and we sort of reintroduced ourselves, because we hadn't really talked much when I'd been on holiday visits.

'I gather you're going to teach me gardening,' I said, making a bit of a face because the idea didn't appeal much, to be honest. He grinned.

'At the moment, if you could just sell Christmas trees, it would be marvellous. Then Paul and I would be free to do the actual gardening and the more difficult sales.

And if you could make holly wreaths — your Grandad had fixed up with a girl to do them, but she let us down. Some flipping florist's offered her more money.'

'I'll have a go,' I promised. Fortunately, I like making things. I'd have time, too. Because it was so close to the Christmas holidays anyway, it had been decided I wouldn't start at the convent school until the start of the new term in January.

Steve told me Paul was working in one of the greenhouses, so I tracked him down and gave him his coffee and cake. He was a bit older than Steve — and very different! While Steve looked like a gardener, tanned and strong with big, capable hands; Paul looked very much like a student, lanky and a bit pale with a thin, intelligent face. But what I just couldn't help noticing was his hair — or rather, that under his woolly hat it didn't look as if he had got any hair to speak of! Just a soft fuzz.

I suppose I must have stared, because he grinned. 'Pondering about the skinhead cut?' he asked. 'We had a sponsored haircut at college — so much per inch, proceeds to charity. I let them go the whole way!'

'Trouble is,' I said, looking at his jeans and anorak, 'the clothes don't match. What you really ought to do is paint your scalp in glowing colours and wear a tasteful little outfit in fluorescent plastic and dustbin bags.'

I suppose it was a bit cheeky of me really, since we'd only just met, but Paul didn't strike me as the sort of person who'd be in the least stuffy or offended. He wasn't — he just laughed.

'Watch it — I might just be mad enough to do it! Students are expected to be mad — it's part of the image, even at a college like mine!'

'What college is it?' I asked, expecting him to say a horticultural one. To my surprise, he looked a bit embarrassed and admitted to attending the Royal College

13

of Music. If I'd gone there, I would have shouted it from the rooftops, because from what I'd heard you had to be a real musical genius to get in! But presumably Paul, freaky hair or no, wasn't such a show-off as me. Still, it explained his hands – not gardener's hands at all, but long and sensitive.

I had to go back then because Mum was calling me but I'd seen enough of Steve and Paul to decide they could be fun to have around – rather like the older brothers I'd always wanted but never had. Not boyfriend material, because they were too old and probably had girlfriends of their own already. But they would make up a bit for losing Andy!

After washing up, I unpacked things in my room and made a big fuss of the cats. My room was super – it must have been a hay store once, when the Nurseries were a house with stables and a coach house attached. They had left the old beams visible when they panelled and ceilinged the room – and it was warm because it was right above the kitchen and the stove chimney went up behind my wall. The walls were panelled with that faced hardboard that looks like wood – very classy, and the cats wouldn't be able to scratch it to bits! My windows looked over the back garden and the river – the airfield was on the other side of the road, at the front.

Best of all, I had masses of space. And perhaps as a sort of consolation prize for having to move, Dad had put his big old writing-desk in my room, together with a stack of paper. There was also a note.

'Just think,' it said, in Dad's familiar scrawl, 'now you'll have some totally different experiences to write about.'

Looked at that way, it did seem a bit more cheerful. No point in crying for the creek anyway – it was gone. Maybe I'd get back there eventually but I couldn't live my life on maybe tomorrows. Now was Stoke Denman, and it was

14

now I was going to have to enjoy.

So I practised a smile in the mirror and went downstairs to lay the table while Mum cooked up an instant-from-frozen dinner. I was tired, and lonely and fed up, but so what? I was also *A Tremayne* — and we always pull through!

CHAPTER 2

THE FAMILY BUSINESS

I woke next morning to the sound of the lorry pulling away and Dad's mates calling their goodbyes. All my tiredness had gone so while Mum was doing breakfast I explored a bit. The back garden was hidden under snow and the river looked just as weedy as I remembered it. But there was ice on it, and though it was too thin for sliding now (it cracked when I thumped it with the heel of my boot), it could be fun when the real hard frosts came. One thing I couldn't do in Cornwall was skate, except when, as a special treat, we went over to the artificial rink in Camborne.

A path led round to the main garden beds, then to the front, where we had quite a big car park, with a boom and chain arrangement you could put across to keep people out when the Nurseries were shut. Around the car park were things like plastic pools, plaster tubs, stone birdbaths and even a few garden gnomes (yuk!). Then more paths led to beds, sheds and greenhouses. Grandad had bought the place when it was going to rack and ruin, putting all his skill and time into it. I dimly remembered, when I was very small, that he'd asked Dad to go into partnership with him, and Dad hadn't wanted to. But now, after all, we were lumbered with being part of the 'family business'. And busy we were, from the word go!

We'd travelled down on a Saturday and the Nurseries didn't open on Sunday, but that didn't mean we had a day of rest. No such luck! For a start, most of the furniture hadn't been put in the way Mum liked it, so we had to shift it around. Then Dad had arranged with Steve to come up specially, to put price tags on things and start making a list of jobs – what had to be done and who did it. He wanted to get things straight before we were busy again on Monday. Steve also tried to teach us how to identify plants – he not only knew them, Latin names and all, but he spoke of them like personal friends and I reckon almost anything would have grown, just to please him! Paul was also hanging around which pleased Dad because he wanted to talk about salaries and conditions and whether he and Steve had been paid properly since Grandad's accident. There were lots of things to sort out, and though Dad had commuted backwards and forwards quite a bit since the crash, he'd mainly fixed up emergency measures until we came down properly. In fact I was pretty vague about what he had been doing – Dad is not that good at talking things over with us! Which was why, when he told Paul and Steve where we stood, it took me by surprise.

'I wouldn't have come into this just on a help-out basis,' he explained. 'It wouldn't have been business-like and could have caused problems later. We are buying the stable block we live in, and have bought a third share in the Nurseries themselves, in partnership with my father. Now, although I know the office side, I know very little about gardening. So I'll be looking to you to teach me.'

So we really had put roots down! Despite what Mum had said, I'd still somehow been thinking of this as a temporary move. Of course, it did make sense to be proper business partners, not helpers who could be thought interfering or, later, dependent relatives! But it must have taken every penny we'd got and quite a bit borrowed from the bank, too – so it certainly meant we were staying.

Then Dad asked Paul to take me round the greenhouses and explain things there, while he spoke to Steve about his job. I flinched at the thought of yet more Latin names, but luckily Paul just showed me how to do the easy things I might have to help with when he went back to college. Like potting out seedlings, and how to take cuttings off easy to grow plants like Busy Lizzies, Fibrous Begonias and that thing with pretty multi-coloured leaves (all right, I've looked it up – Coleus). Then Dad came in.

'Just been sorting out days off and what have you with Steve,' he explained. 'What are your days off, Paul? Or what would you like?'

'Just Thursday – and Sunday, of course, when we're shut anyway,' Paul said. 'I'd like to keep the Thursday, because I go up for flute and piano lessons.'

'Would you like, say, a half-day on Saturdays too, so you can go home at weekends?'

A kind of shuttered look came into Paul's eyes. 'Frankly, the less I see of my parents, the better for all concerned,' he said quietly. 'I'm afraid we don't exactly get on. I'd better go and see them on Christmas Day, but for the rest, I'm just as happy staying here.'

I got the feeling I was listening into a conversation I probably shouldn't hear, so I drifted away to see if Mum wanted any help. But I was curious. I have my arguments with Mum and Dad (who doesn't?) but I couldn't imagine wanting to avoid them. Whatever was up between Paul and his parents had to be pretty serious. Perhaps it was his hair? But surely having your hair cut off to help a good cause wouldn't upset any sensible parent? In fact, when I'd told my Mum about it, she'd laughed.

Mysterious! But by lunchtime I'd almost forgotten. I was so starving all I could think about was food. And we stayed on safe subjects during the meal, like – how did you guess? Gardens and gardening! Steve told us how he'd grown up with plants, as his family for generations had been Head Gardeners at the Manor.

'When it was a Manor,' he added ruefully. 'The family who had lived there for centuries finally realized they couldn't afford it any more, and sold it last year. It's a Conference Centre now, which has brought some work to the village. But Dad lost out – they decided to use a gardening contract firm. And they go to a florist in Wycombe for all their flowers and plants for functions.'

'A pity,' Dad commented. 'We could do with their business.'

'You seemed busy enough when we arrived,' I said, but Steve shook his head.

'This is just the pre-Christmas rush. It'll ease off a lot afterwards. Really, we need something new and different – a speciality that will attract people. We've got a lot of competition in this area and we just can't compete properly with the ones who have a lot of money and can keep stocks of swimming pool equipment, have fancy tools and special hothouses for orchids, things like that.'

'Well, I'm afraid we're not exactly financial wizards,' Dad admitted, 'but never mind, we usually struggle through. Now, do you think we could just go over the spring planting programme?'

Not with me they couldn't; I'd had enough! So I nobly offered to do the washing and wiping up, then skived off to my room for a bit of reading and actually managed to get a couple of hours of peace until Dad and the boys came in wanting a cup of tea. While we were having this, a rather worried looking lady with twin toddlers in tow knocked on our door.

'I hate to disturb you when you've only just moved in and I know you're shut,' she said anxiously, 'but I've done something dreadful . . .'

'Come in, Mrs Burnett!' Dad exclaimed, and then of course we had introductions all round, and Mum thanking her for the cake and saying she was sorry she hadn't come over to say thanks but she'd been so busy. You know, all the usual polite noises!

The dreadful thing Mrs Burnett had done was not really so awful – she'd not murdered anyone in their beds, just forgotten to order a holly wreath which she'd promised to bring to help decorate the village hall for a carol concert that evening. Apparently they had it every year – a few special items, and lots of carols for the audience to join in. Old and housebound local people were brought in cars, and a busload from the nearest old people's home also came. They were given tea in another bit of the hall before the concert. There was no evening service in the church because the Vicar acted as compère and the organist played. (Good job she told us – we'd planned to go to church that night!)

'It's a real village get-together,' she said. 'Why don't you come! You'd meet a lot of local people. We're all going, and you could come back and have coffee or a drink with us afterwards. I'm sure your Fran and my Celia would get on marvellously together.'

I'd almost forgotten that-nice-girl-Celia-you-can-be-friends-with, and I must admit I wasn't too pleased at the way both our mums seemed determined to match us up! I like to make my own friends. But Dad heard Mrs Burnett too.

'Thanks very much, we'd like that,' he said, watching me to make sure I looked suitably pleased. I looked away and pretended to be keeping an eye on the little kids, who were dangerously fascinated by a pile of plates Mum hadn't yet got round to putting away.

'Now, that wreath – I'm sure we can do something,' Mum said. 'What would you like?'

'Anything simple would do – a bit of holly and something colourful . . . Sammy! Sue! How many times do I have to tell you not to touch . . . naughty!'

20

The plates teetered and I caught hold of them just in time. The twins obviously thought it was all very funny, but I couldn't help feeling sorry for Mrs Burnett!

'I'll make something,' I promised, 'though it may not be very professional. Shall I run it over to the airfield, or shall we take it with us?'

'I'll send Mike or Celia over for it at about five-thirty, if that's OK. Thanks very much,' she said, in relief. Dad offered her some greenery for the hall, free, if she or her husband would like to collect and cut it − our private bit of garden was overflowing with evergreens and berried bushes.

'I'll get my husband to come over with Mike,' she promised. Then, thanking us again, she dragged her twins away before they could have another go at demolishing the plates.

She'd hardly been gone ten minutes when her husband arrived, with a boy of about sixteen who turned out to be Mike. They borrowed secateurs and a little saw, vanished into our garden and emerged a bit later with their arms full of greenery. They'd made quite a neat job of trimming our bushes! I offered them coffee, but they said they had to get back, so I staggered in and made one for myself. What with all the comings and goings, the new things to learn and do, all the people I had to try and sort out in my mind, I was getting tired and confused and a bit edgy. I wished we could have settled in gently, not been thrown in at the deep end like this, and I just couldn't help feeling resentful and grumbly. Life in Peveran had followed a pattern, a nice pattern which I'd got used to ever since I was a little kid. Oh, I'd known I would one day grow up, and maybe move away − in fact I'd daydreamed about travelling the world − but I hadn't wanted or expected a whole load of changes just to be dumped on me, whether I liked them or not.

21

I wanted to curl up on my bed with a book but I had to make the wreath I'd promised for Mrs Burnett, so I dragged myself out in search of chicken wire, and found some in an untidy heap in one of the sheds. Guessing, I made a ring of wire bound over on itself, sealing the sharp bits with sticky tape and stuffing the lot with sphagnum moss. Then I raided our gardens and the Nurseries for different kinds of holly, a few Christmas roses, some fir cones, and winter jasmine, which I threaded or tied in place. As always, making things helped me relax and by teatime I was feeling fairly cheerful and pleased with myself, because the wreath didn't look at all bad. And Steve reckoned he could get his aunt, who'd been to floral art classes, to come up the next day to give me tips on stuff you could use, and how to keep flowers fresh.

'Well done,' Dad approved. 'Do you reckon you could do a few more tomorrow? We'll come to some arrangement regarding extra pocket money.'

'I'll do them!' I promised eagerly. Though I had the Mirror money, I wanted to use it for something special, and I still had Christmas presents to buy, so extra cash would come in handy.

'And I'm afraid I've got an extra job for you tomorrow, Paul,' Dad warned. 'When I visited my Dad this afternoon, he said something about sending trees to hospitals each year.'

'Grief!' Steve yelled, thumping himself on the head. 'I forgot! Yes — there's two to local hospitals and two to London hospitals. They'll be wondering what has happened. Mr Tremayne always gave them the biggest and best we had.'

'I was thinking Paul could take them in the van, tomorrow afternoon. You do have a licence, don't you?' asked Dad.

Paul nodded, looking pleased. 'I'll be glad of a chance

to get into London,' he admitted. 'I need to pick up some stuff from the hostel.'

'Paul might need a hand with the trees,' I said hopefully. I hadn't been to London since I was ten, when a load of us from the village went up on a special train, had four hours for Christmas shopping, then back again. London's so far from Cornwall, it might have been a foreign country! But of course, from Stoke Denman it was only an hour or so's journey away.

'If you get the wreaths done in the morning, you can go with Paul and have a look at the lights,' Dad promised. 'Though I doubt if there'll be time for shopping.'

But I didn't actually want to buy anything — just to go along Oxford Street and Regent Street, gawping in the windows and thinking what I would buy if I were rich. So it was settled Paul would take the local trees first and I'd help — then we'd come back for the other two and go off to London. With that all worked out, we settled down to the serious business of having tea, and we'd just about finished when Mike arrived for the wreath. Funny, I'd never really noticed him, the times I'd come down on visits — I suppose he'd been off with his friends somewhere, or over at the airfield.

Hoping he might turn out to be another Andy, I started chatting to him but once he'd learned I didn't fly and didn't even have a burning ambition to fly, he wasn't interested. Flying was his big thing, obviously. He was in Air Cadets, did gliding, and was aiming to fly one of his Dad's planes as soon as he was old enough. He also wanted to do parachuting, parascending, and hang-gliding. To be honest, he struck me as a bit of a bighead (though I can talk!), full of what *he* did and what *he* intended to do. When I said I'd like someone to take me for a flight, just to see what it was like, but I didn't think I'd ever dare go solo because I'd be sure to crash the plane onto a school or something awful, he just gave me a pitying smirk, writing me off as a feeble girl. And I'm not!

'What about your sister Celia?' I asked. 'Is she keen on flying too?'

'Not her!' he said contemptuously. 'She's obsessed with ballet. Bores us all to tears with ballet, ballet and wanting to go to White Lodge, the boarding school for future prima ballerinas.'

'Perhaps you *have* to be obsessed, with something like ballet,' I suggested, 'or you'd never stand the work and the discipline.'

Privately, I began to feel cross with Mike, and a bit sorry for Celia. Instant judgement, I know, but I got the feeling that because his Dad ran the flying school, it was OK for Mike to waffle on about flying as much as he liked. But as nobody else in the family was into ballet, as soon as Celia tried to talk about *her* dreams, everyone switched her off as boring. It's awful if nobody shares your interests, and thinks you're a bit peculiar for having them in the first place! Anyway, it occurred to me that if I was Celia, I wouldn't like people discussing me behind my back, so I just shut up and got the wreath and Mike took it away. I don't think either of us had impressed the other very much, and when Mum asked me hopefully how I'd got on with Mike Burnett, I shrugged. 'I don't think he'd be interested in me unless I grow wings.'

'Never mind,' Mum said. 'You'll probably get on beautifully with Celia, and there's sure to be some other young people in and around the village. Perhaps you'll get to meet some at the carol concert tonight.'

Privately, I didn't hold out much hope. I was back in a sulky mood again. Now, on a Peveran Sunday I would have had a super afternoon with my friends and a carol concert would have been fun — I'd probably have been in it . . .

24

'For goodness' sake, Fran, stop mooching around like a depressed dishrag!' Dad snapped. 'Go and have a bath, and change into something decent. And hurry!'

'Christmas!' I muttered 'Peace and goodwill . . .'

But I did as I was told. I didn't like the way I was feeling at all, all cross and mixed up inside, up one minute, down the next. I'd never felt like that before. Normally, I'm a pretty cheerful type. It had to be the moving! Anyway, I borrowed Mum's scented bubble bath and sang at the top of my voice while the water ran, which cheered me up a bit and I was feeling fairly human by the time we were ready to go.

Steve was going too, but he'd gone home to change first. He liked slopping around in his working clothes but he said his girlfriend would clobber him if he turned up looking scruffy. Paul wasn't going at all. We offered to take him, but he said a polite no thanks, and as we left I could hear him playing his flute. I thought he'd have wanted to go, being so musical, and for a moment I felt cross with him − perhaps he thought he was too good for a mere amateur village concert! But it wasn't that at all − Mum told me quietly that Paul wasn't a Christian so he thought it would be hypocritical for him to sing carols. And she hinted strongly that I shouldn't try to get him in arguments about it, either!

We crawled the two miles to the village proper, because it was snowing again, and Dad wasn't used to it and didn't know the road well. But we made it, fifteen minutes before the concert was due to start. The church was pure Christmas card, with a lych-gate and walls of mellowed stone. The hall, next to it, was very different − a rather ugly new building, but it was warm and friendly inside. The vicar greeted us at the door and introduced us to some people whose names I promptly forgot, but who seemed nice and friendly. Some of them, like the vicar, recognized

25

Dad from his flying visits after the accident, and all of them asked after Grandad. He was obviously well liked and they were all worried about him.

Mr Burnett came over, and said he'd saved seats for us with him, Celia and the twins. Mrs Burnett was singing in the choir and Mike was sitting with his friend Peter. So we went with Mr Burnett and I met Celia properly at last. My vague memories of her had been of a thin, dark-haired girl; but she wasn't skinny-thin, just slender and fine-boned. If Mike hadn't told me about her ballet, I think I would have guessed anyway, because she looked like a dancer, especially with her long black hair drawn back into a kind of bun. She smiled at me shyly and I smiled back. I know it sounds stupid, but with everyone expecting us to be friends, I think we were both a bit wary and didn't know what to say. Then one of the twins broke the ice for us by starting to stroke the fur collar of the lady in front. As Celia hastily stopped him and apologized to the lady, I told her how the twins had done their best to topple mum's plates.

'I bet they drive you barmy sometimes!' I said, and she laughed.

'You can say that again – they're into everything! Mum's always terrified they'll run in front of a plane or something, but planes seem to be the one thing they understand. It's plates and plants and supermarket displays that they specialize in demolishing.'

'I used to wish I had brothers and sisters,' I admitted, 'but sometimes I'm glad I don't. Friends are much better – I hope we can be friends. It'd be great having a friend on my doorstep, especially going to my school. I'm not really looking forward to starting a new school.'

I found myself telling her about my friends in Peveran, and how I missed them. Then it suddenly occurred to me that she might have plenty of friends of her own already, and not want me butting in.

'Oh, you won't be, honest!' she said hastily. 'There's quite a lot of little kids in the village, but hardly anyone our age. And the two girls who are, Kate and Jenny, go to boarding school so I only see them in the holidays. And my friends at school are boarders, so I only see them in the term, and then I feel a bit left out because they talk about things they do in the dorms, secret suppers and things. It'd be great to have a friend both inside and outside school. You don't — you wouldn't do ballet, by any chance?'

' 'fraid not,' I admitted. 'But I love to watch it.'

She smiled then and visibly relaxed. 'Mum and Dad were hoping I'd make friends with you, so you'd wean me off ballet. They can't understand why I like it so much, it doesn't mean a thing to them.'

'And I reckon my Mum and Dad were hoping I'd make friends with you, so I'd stop missing my old friends and going into the sulks!'

We both giggled. With both sets of parents pushing us to be friends, we should have hated each other on sight! But I decided I could quite get to like Celia and obviously she thought the same about me. The concert was about to start (a bit late) so I suggested that we had the twins between us, so we could each keep an eye on one. Gratefully, she took Sammy while I took Sue, but once the singing started, they were good as gold anyway.

There were a few nuns in the seats opposite, and some girls in convent school uniform — my future teachers and schoolmates. I was relieved to see they looked reasonably normal!

By the third carol I had relaxed completely, all my bad moods gone, and was able to let the joy of Christmas flow around and into me. The fun of being a Christian hadn't

27

got left behind in Peveran after all – it was here, too, as we sang all the old favourite carols, and the Drama Club acted out the lovely story of the Fourth Wise Man. A kids' recorder group murdered two carols, but even that didn't matter – they looked sweet! And the concert ended with the choir, loud and triumphant, singing 'Unto us a child is born, unto us a son is given,' while the village children marched up to put their gifts for a childrens' charity on the stage. At this, the twins came to noisy life because they wanted to go up too – Sam had some gooey toffees in his pocket which he wanted to give and Sue, not to be outdone, had a lolly with bits of fluff sticking to it.

'It's the thought that counts!' I whispered to Celia, who grinned and nodded, so we each took a twin up to leave their 'gifts'. The vicar thanked them gravely.

Afterwards there was tea and mince pies for everyone in a side room, but we were only able to stay a few minutes, because the Burnetts had invited us back and they had to leave early as it was already well past the twins' bedtime. So we said our goodbyes and trudged off into the snow. Although it wasn't more than an inch deep the car wheels whirred a bit as we started off, and Dad said we'd need to put chains and sacks and bits of old carpet in the boot, in case we got stuck at any time.

'Still, a white Christmas will be fun,' Mum said. 'I'll get a lot of shopping in tomorrow, build up a store cupboard for emergencies. And I must go down to the Post Office. What nice people they are here – I've already been invited to the WI's Christmas Party.'

'I'll have to find something to join, once Christmas is over,' I thought aloud. I'd been involved in so much in Peveran!

'There'll be plenty of activities connected with your school,' Mum assured me.

I didn't really fancy school-type activities in my spare

time, but I didn't say so. It might be better to wait and see what they were. At a push, I could even take up ballet, like Celia, or join Air Cadets, like Mike — if they took girls. Not that I was able to ask him that night — he hadn't come home with his parents, but had asked if he could go with Peter and walk back from his house later. I had a nasty feeling he didn't want to have to make polite conversation with me and his sister — well, blow him!

Celia and I joined in the parental chat for a while, then we escaped to her room and I asked her about the school. She was pretty enthusiastic and it didn't sound nearly as strict and grim as I'd feared it would be — quite the opposite, in fact. Nobody expected you to turn into a saint overnight. And as Mum had guessed, there were lots of societies — Drama, Debating, Music, Riding. There was no sailing club, but then how could they have one, when there wasn't anywhere decent to sail?

'Do you do ballet at school?' I asked, and she shook her head. That, apparently, was the big problem. She didn't *really* want to go to White Lodge — in fact she said honestly that she was sure she wasn't even good enough. But she did desperately want more ballet lessons.

'At present I only get two hours a week, in Wycombe, on Saturday mornings,' she sighed. 'I can't go to evening lessons because there's no buses and Mum and Dad won't run me in. There's always something more important, or no time, or Mum can't leave the twins. But it's a different story when Mike has to go to Air Cadets and he can't get a lift with Peter for some reason. They'll run him in, then!'

'But that's downright sex discrimination!' I said indignantly.

Celia sighed. 'No, not really. It's not because he's a boy — it's just that they think flying is useful. I mean, they hope Mike will go through all his licences, and eventually run the flying school when Dad wants

29

to retire. But they can't see any use for ballet at all!'

'Of course it's useful! It gives a lot of fun to a lot of people. I'd like to see you dance.'

'Really?' Celia's big, dark brown eyes lit up with pleasure. 'My ballet school's doing their Winter Show on Tuesday evening,' she said eagerly. 'I could get you a ticket and you could have a lift in with me — to be on the safe side, my teacher's fetching me and bringing me home. Mum says she'll come and I've got her ticket but it'll only take one of the twins to play up or be sick, and she'll stay home with them.'

'Yes, please, I'd love to come,' I enthused. Not that I was really all that keen, but I reckoned Celia was getting a raw deal and deserved some encouragement. So that was all arranged and when we went downstairs chatting, I saw our mothers exchanging glances that said, 'There, isn't that nice, the girls have made friends.' I wonder if they'd have been so happy if they'd known I'd just made a resolution to Help Celia Get Her Rights?

CHAPTER 3

FAMOUS LAST WORDS

By the next morning the snow was quite deep. But they were obviously used to bad weather because the roads had already been cleared and gritted when I went down to breakfast. Maybe Mr Burnett did our little country lane – he had a snowplough attachment on a tractor for clearing the runways because they went flying every day unless the weather was actually dangerous. When the wind was northerly, planes took off more or less over our house; but though I heard them often that morning, I didn't get time to watch them!

Steve's aunt turned up as promised and I made wreaths while she helped. Then she gave me a crash course in basic floral arrangements – nothing fancy, just what people would expect for bouquets, posies and wreaths. Then after lunch we put one tree in the van (bending the top a bit and even so it pricked me) and another on the roof, dropped them off to the local hospitals, then loaded another two and shot off to London. Well, not exactly shot – what with the weather and the van not being his, Paul drove pretty carefully. And we didn't take the van right into the heart of London either. The hospitals were on the outskirts and, after delivering the trees, we went round to Paul's hostel where he picked up a file bulging with paper, and a guitar. Then he looked at his watch.

'Only four-thirty,' he said. 'Shall I ring your Dad and ask if he'd mind if we parked the van, and got the underground into Oxford Street for a quick look at the shops?'

'Yes, please!'

'I don't fancy driving. London drivers are crazy!'

'The underground's fine by me,' I agreed, remembering how when I was a kid, we came up for a pantomime but I wanted to do nothing but ride up and down the escalators all day! I still liked them!

Luckily, Dad said we could stay on a bit, so long as we got home by 8 p.m. at the latest, and brought fish and chips with us because Mum was visiting Grandad and couldn't cook an evening meal.

So we parked the van and soon were standing sardine-packed on an underground train, heading first for Trafalgar Square to see the huge fir tree from Norway. Living in Peveran, I'd almost forgotten what real crowds were like and London was so busy it scared and excited me at the same time. I could see what Paul meant about the traffic – I reckon a nervous driver stuck in the wrong lane would just have to go on driving right out of London and then try again!

There were people of every nationality under the sun, all looking at the sights and the shops – and some moving very quickly through the crowds, city workers eager to catch their trains home. Paul flowed in and out of the people as if this was his natural habitat, exclaiming and pointing things out to me. I just tried to keep him in sight, because if I lost him, I wouldn't have had a clue how to get to his hostel! We didn't go into any of the shops, but we did buy some hot chestnuts, and I got some flowers from a barrow for Mum (which come to think of it, was a bit like taking coals to Newcastle!). Then Paul said we'd better be getting back.

We were delayed a bit at the hostel because some of his friends, who'd been out when we left the van, had come back and of course they invited us in for coffee. I didn't enjoy that much, to be honest. The coffee tasted like ditchwater and the boys all talked music and shared happenings which I knew nothing about. Two things made me prick up my ears — a remark one of them made to Paul about 'the demo' and another about 'his masterpiece' — but before I could get a word in to ask what demo and what masterpiece, they were rabbiting on about something else! And boys have the cheek to say *girls* talk too much!

Anyway, we had to go. So in the van coming home I asked Paul about the 'masterpiece'. (Some little voice inside warned me to go easy on the 'demo', and it was right!)

He grinned. 'Oh, it's just this rock opera I'm trying to write. Masterpiece it isn't, you don't want to take any notice of those two idiots!'

'What's it about?'

He shrugged. I think he was half embarrassed, but the other half, that wanted to talk about it, won. 'Oh, peace, love, brotherhood,' he said a bit awkwardly. 'I reckon we've got to learn to get on together before we blow our world to bits. Or destroy it by ruining the ecology. So I'm trying to say it in music because I reckon people listen more to music. If you just talk at them, they think you're some kind of a nut and switch off.'

Then, scared he was getting too serious, I suppose, he grinned. 'Anyway, it's good practice.'

'Sing me a bit,' I urged, but he wasn't keen because he said it really needed the instruments and the right voices. But I kept on at him, until he eventually gave in and sang the opening number.

Well, I admit I've heard better singers, but I don't think I've ever heard a better song! For starters, it had a super rhythm that made me want to get up and dance (not easy in a van going down the motorway!). And — oh, it got down inside me somehow. There was one line that kept on being repeated, so you could guess where it was coming, and long before the end I was joining in with 'I believe in Planet Earth!'. I could imagine a whole audience not just sitting there, but getting up and dancing, then all shouting together 'I believe in Planet Earth!'.

When Paul finished he didn't look at me, just kept his eyes on the road as if he was scared I'd say it was awful. When I clapped and said I thought it was brilliant, he relaxed a bit and I got him to sing another. This was different (he said it was meant to have a lot of weird electronic sounds in the background). Even without them it was a bit scarey.

By now, though, I was impressed. I'd never realized music students could do rock — I'd just imagined them being into Beethoven and classical stuff. And I suppose Paul's music wasn't pure rock — that first song had had a bit of folk in it, and one he tried to sing later had some opera too. But all the music fitted together — I felt it was grabbing me, shaking me, making me want to get involved in what it was saying. It certainly wasn't something I could play in the background while I did my homework!

The words were good, too — in some songs the words are rubbish. But Paul had written the sort of things I like to write myself, and he'd done it so well it almost made me feel jealous. What on earth was a Pure Genius doing flogging Christmas trees and potting out Busy Lizzies in our Nurseries?

'You ought to put it on in the West End,' I assured him. 'Honest, it's brilliant.'

Paul grinned. 'Well, thanks for the vote of confidence, but theatrical impresarios don't exactly fight for the chance to put on work by unknown music students,' he said, wryly.

'Well, if the rest is as good as the bits you've sung to me, it ought to be performed somehow, somewhere,' I insisted. 'Couldn't you get your music student friends to perform it, at college?'

'They'd do it, all right, but I'm not exactly the college's blue-eyed boy at the moment. Rock's not their favourite music and anyway, I haven't nearly finished it yet. It's probably just a bright idea that will never happen, or will turn sour somewhere – I've had those before.'

Suddenly, Paul looked very small and lonely, in the half-light of the van. Younger, and so uncertain I wanted to mother him! And he obviously didn't want to talk about his rock opera any more because he firmly changed the subject. For the rest of the way home we talked about sledging and skating, safe things like that. We picked up fish and chips in Wycombe and our timing was just right because on the last stretch home we saw Mum's car in front of us, and we pulled in to the Nurseries together.

Steve had gone home, so it was just Mum and Dad, Paul and me, tucking into fish and chips, while the cats hovered round yelling for a share – they'll steal or scrounge anything they can, even though we feed them well. It's partly my fault; I can't resist giving them little bits though Mum tells me not to!

I asked how Grandad was and she said he was much better, and that she'd promised either she or Dad would take me in to see him the next day.

'He's raring to get out of bed and start doing things, take up life again,' she said. 'There's no way he'll accept the doctors' verdict that he shouldn't do much.'

'That's great,' Paul and I said together.

'He's certainly not the type to give up and do nothing,' Dad said. 'We must try and think of some way he can be happily occupied without trying to kill himself by doing too much.'

I thought for a bit, then came up with an idea I'd actually pinched from Stella, a disabled friend of mine (we met when she came down on holiday to Peveran with some other disabled kids). 'Raised gardens for people in wheelchairs and old people who can't bend down to weed,' I suggested. 'He could look after them and show them off, and it might be something different the other nurseries haven't got.'

Dad looked quite impressed. 'Not a bad idea, Fran. What do you think, Paul?'

'A good idea — I should imagine we could make a few simple raised beds with breeze-blocks or bricks. But Steve is the real expert — better ask him.'

Dad promised he would, in the morning, and after that Paul went back to his bedsitter. I wanted to talk before I went to bed, so I curled up in an armchair opposite Mum, who was knitting, and told her about Paul's rock opera. I also asked her if she had any idea what had happened between his parents and him.

'No, I don't,' she said. 'And it's none of our business really, is it? I suppose most families have their problems with the generation gap.'

'Except us,' I said happily. 'I reckon we do very well!'

Ever heard the saying, 'famous last words'? Because next day we had the biggest family bust-up for ages . . .

Most of the day went off fine. I helped at the Nurseries in the morning and in the afternoon Mum took me in to see Grandad. Although I was a bit shocked to see how old, ill and frail he looked, I felt sure he was going to be all right — and he quite liked the idea of a Wheelchair Garden.

'New blood means new, young ideas — just what we need,' he said. 'Settling in all right?'

I couldn't tell him a couple of days wasn't long enough to know, or that I still felt pretty lost, confused, cross and lonely sometimes. It would only have worried him, so I said everything was great, I was getting on fine with Paul and Steve, and had made friends with Celia.

'Nice girl,' he approved. 'Thought I must admit I like her brother more — he's got a lot of get-up-and-go.'

I was surprised he liked Mike, but I didn't say that I thought he was a show-off without a thought in his thick head except planes. I told him instead about how we'd taken the trees to the hospitals, and gone to London and we ended up talking about practically everything except his accident and his injuries. He mentioned that only once, when I said something nasty about the drunken driver. Grandad said he felt sorry for the man — apparently his wife had left him, then his son had died of leukemia, and he'd just fallen apart at the seams.

'I just hope they don't send him to prison,' he said. 'After all, I'm going to be OK. Those young doctors think just because I'm not in my first youth any more I'm some frail hot-house plant. They don't know us Tremaynes, eh? Before you know where you are, I'll be home again, bossing the lot of you about!'

I could believe it, too!

Sometimes hospital visiting is really draggy but with Grandad the time went all too quickly, then Mum was there to run me home. She'd agreed I could go to Celia's ballet show, and I needed to eat and change first. The ballet teacher was collecting us at 6 p.m. though the show didn't start until 7.30 p.m. Celia, having a solo part in it, had to get there in good time to put on her costume and make-up. She promised I could come backstage and help her, rather than have to sit around waiting in the empty theatre, and I was quite looking forward to it.

At just before six, I ran across to the airfield, to Celia's big house. She was pacing up and down their living room, looking out of the window for her teacher's car, and she had a very bad case of stage fright.

'I love it when I'm actually dancing,' she wailed. 'If only I didn't feel so scared and sick first. I keep having this

37

awful urge to burp! I'm sure something is going to go horribly wrong . . .'

Mike was bending over the table, putting the finishing touch to a model aircraft (Tuesday was one of his Air Cadet nights). 'For pity's sake,' he moaned. 'Anyone would think it was Covent Garden, not a little ballet school show to a crowd of devoted mums. And if you get so uptight about it, why do it?'

'Oh, you wouldn't understand! I don't suppose you ever get nervous about going up in your beloved gliders!'

'Oh, yes I do! But I don't insist on telling everyone about it non-stop for three hours.'

'I'm not having a pianist, my music is on tape and it'll be absolutely awful if they get it in the wrong place and nothing happens or I get the wrong music.'

I tried to reassure her. 'You can always improvise if that does happen, but it won't. They'll have got it down to a fine art by now.'

'Miss Field ought to be here by now. What if her car's broken down?'

Mike sighed and went to the window. 'She is due at six,' he said heavily. 'It is now 5.56 and there are headlights coming down the road.'

Luckily, it was Miss Field, who was young and pretty. Unluckily, she was just as strung up with nerves as Celia, though for a different reason − she was in charge of the youngest kids, who were doing an Animal Ballet right at the beginning of the show.

'And if anything goes wrong for them,' she said grimly, 'they have a habit of sitting on stage bawling their eyes out, or jumping off it and running to Mum in the audience. And they're so busy looking at their families, that they forget what they're supposed to be doing!'

Eventually, I ended up trying to calm the pair of them down. And when we actually arrived at the theatre and went backstage, it was even worse – everyone from the littlest Baby Bunny to the accompanist who'd lost some of her music was running round in circles getting in a right old panic. I concentrated on helping Celia into her costume, a space-age glittery thing in stretch fabric, and putting on her equally futuristic make-up. She was doing a modern dance she'd choreographed herself, which was an extra reason for being nervous – it was the first time the school had allowed any pupil to do that. I was quite sorry when I had to leave her and go out front – I had a feeling she wanted someone to hold her hand until the very minute she went on stage! It would have helped, perhaps, if she could have been sure her Mum would turn up, but her seat next to me was still empty when the curtain went up. But she arrived after the tinies' Animal Ballet had finished.

'Mike went to Peter's and Peter had forgotten to tell him that he and his Dad were going somewhere that night – darts match or something – so he couldn't have a lift. Then of course I had to run him into Air Cadets . . .' she whispered. Typical! More and more I began to think Mike was spoilt *rotten*!

'You haven't missed Celia's dance,' I assured her. 'It's number three – "Ark to the Stars, danced and choreographed by Celia Burnett".'

First, we had to sit through a rather ghastly *pas de deux* by a boy and girl who thought they were Fonteyn and Nureyev and weren't. Then the curtains opened to the first notes of the *Space Odyssey* theme music and Celia was on.

Now, sometimes when people go on a lot about the things they want to do, it makes you wonder if they're all hot air and you start to wonder if they can actually *do* what they're talking about. I think that was probably what had happened to Celia with her family, especially as they didn't like ballet much anyway. But I was watching with an open mind, and even though I don't know much about ballet, I could see she was good. She wasn't doing classical stuff, all balancing on points and arabesques, but she had this kind of modern style which used a lot of mime, some almost gymnastic movements and was terrifically expressive. I knew what she was dancing – she was a starship captain, perhaps the last spaceship from Earth or maybe one from another planet. Behind her as she danced a stream of kids, some just people, some animals, moved slowly. She was guiding them onto the ship, offering them hope, a new chance in the stars. Paul would have loved it! When it was over, I clapped like mad.

I turned to Mrs Burnett and told her forcibly that Celia was great – maybe even a genius! She just looked astonished and a bit doubtful. 'Well, she's certainly quite clever at dancing,' she admitted, 'but, I mean, this is just a little town ballet school show – I don't imagine she could hold her own in something big and important. And ballet is hopeless as a career – there are so many girls who want to do it, so few jobs, and most will have had much more tuition than her.'

'And whose fault is that?' I wanted to say, but didn't. I knew what she was getting at, though – she didn't want me to encourage Celia, because she didn't think there was any future in ballet for her, only disappointment and discouragement.

Still, she congratulated Celia afterwards, and Celia was thrilled her Mum had made it. She babbled on happily in the car as we drove to pick up Mike – all about the things that had gone right, and the things that had gone very wrong, like one bit of scenery sticking and the elastic giving way in someone's knickers. But she quietened down as we neared the place where we were to pick up Mike – at least half a mile from where the Air Cadets met, because he thought it was downright embarrassing, being brought and picked up by his Mum, and wouldn't let her appear near the hall!

'He wants to cycle to the nearest bus stop, then bus in,' Mrs Burnett explained, 'but I don't think cyclists are visible enough at night. And he can't wait to get a moped – but wait he must. Don't be taken in by the age he pretends to be sometimes, Fran, he's not sixteen yet.'

She sighed. 'I must admit I'd rather he didn't have any kind of motorbike at all until he's at least eighteen, but his father will let him – Mike is very much Dave's son and heir and can do no wrong. And he can afford it because the rich godfather after whom we so tactfully named him, has left money in trust for him, and he's allowed to draw a certain amount each year.'

'Mike,' Celia muttered, 'has jam on it, all the way. Why didn't you get me rich godparents?'

Then of course we had to stop talking about him, because we'd drawn to a halt and he was actually getting in – grousing, because we were fifteen minutes late and he was cold.

But at least he did have the grace to ask Celia how her show had gone, and she said OK. But she didn't say much more about it as we drove home – I suppose she thought he might take the mickey. Though actually, he was suprisingly quiet. Then after a bit he said, 'Thanks for running me in, Mum. I could thump Peter for forgetting to tell me that he and his Dad would be going out – he knew tonight was special. But just lately all he's really interested in is birds and booze! He's been my friend since we were five but he won't be much longer, if he doesn't watch it. Pity you didn't bring a brother down with you, Fran.'

So he could be lonely too! It made me warm to him a bit. But not much!

We got home at about ten-thirty and I admit I was really tired. I'd enjoyed my day but I couldn't wait to get to bed. As Mrs Burnett pulled in outside the Nurseries to drop me before turning in to the airfield, she said that she was going shopping in Aylesbury the next day, and as Celia had now broken up, perhaps we would both like to go in with her and have a swim in the big indoor pool? Mike had still one more day at school so he couldn't come. I said yes, of course, then remembered I'd have to ask Mum and Dad — but I thought that would just be a formality, why should they mind me going? So I told Mrs Burnett I'd run over and let her know for sure first thing in the morning.

Then I went in, found Mum and Dad in their nightclothes ready for bed too, gave them a quick run-down about Celia's show and then asked if I could go swimming.

Which was where everything went wrong.

'No, Fran, you can't,' Mum said. 'Sorry, but there are six wreaths ordered from today, and I won't have time to make them. I'm not as good at it as you, and I've got the house, shopping, hospital visiting and helping with the trees.'

I'd honestly thought, since I became a Christian, I'd grown out of my temper — well, most of it, anyway. At least it had slowed down! But now, perhaps because I was tired, I hit the ceiling.

'Why did you promise them?' I exploded. 'Without asking me if I could make them? What am I, a flipping slave? You don't even pay me, except for a few measly extra pence pocket money.'

'No,' Dad said, quietly. 'And we won't, because at the moment we can't afford to. We're struggling, Fran. We need all the takings we can get, and we expect you to pull your weight, not act like a spoiled brat. At

42

your age, you should be a responsible member of the family.'

'One-sided responsibility,' I snapped back. 'When nobody tells me things or involves me – I just get lumbered with your decisions, then you expect me to be happy about it!'

I said a lot more too – I can't remember all of it, which is probably just as well, because it was pretty awful. Then I burst into tears and slammed out of the room, up into my bedroom to cry myself to sleep at the unfairness of life. Only I couldn't *get* to sleep.

I knew I'd been rude, also that I was sulking – but for a while I just lay there telling myself I had a perfect right to sulk. I knew I'd survive without one swim, and I knew I wasn't being very sensible and grown-up about it – but then Mum and Dad hadn't been fair to me. They couldn't seem to make up their minds what I was supposed to be – a kid who had to do as she was told, or a 'responsible' adult. Nobody had ever consulted *me* about the family money going into partnership – I never knew the least bit about family finances, usually, until Mum and Dad knocked one of my pet dreams on the head by saying we couldn't afford it. Then I was expected to take their decision obediently and cheerfully. Maybe I did take them for granted sometimes, but they took me for granted too. I knew kids at school who didn't lift a finger in the house (while I always had my share of work to do) and got chauffeured everywhere by doting parents (I should be so lucky!). I didn't have any real ambition to be a spoilt brat, but I did think, if Mum and Dad expected me to pull my weight as a 'responsible' adult, they might have the decency to treat me like one, not expect me to be a working part of Tremayne's Nurseries without a real clue what was going on. No wonder employees went on strike if bosses acted like Mum and Dad!

Oh, I had reason to be angry, all right; but deep inside I knew I'd been wrong, too. I shouldn't have blown up and been rude. The more I thought about it, the more ashamed of myself I got, and I knew that if Mum and Dad hadn't gone to bed yet (and I hadn't heard them come upstairs) I'd have to go down and apologize. Not grovel or anything, but apologize for the things I'd said and done that had been wrong. I wouldn't have to expect them to apologize for their wrong bits either — they might, but I knew from past experience that parents seem to have this authority hang-up and find it ever so difficult to say sorry first. That bugged me too, but I'd just have to put up with it!

But I wanted to say more than sorry — I wanted to suggest something to get things working better in the future, and it suddenly occurred to me how I could start. I still had most of my Mirror money — what if I offered to buy a small share in the Nurseries! It might help Mum and Dad, and it would certainly show that as long as I felt involved, I really would pull my weight.

When I get an idea, I have to put it into action fast. I hurried downstairs — then paused outside the door. Mum and Dad were talking. In fact, Mum was telling Dad off — and herself!

'Well, she's right. We haven't been really open with her. She's just been expected to fall in line with our decisions.'

'She is a child!' Dad said indignantly. 'I doubt if she'd understand the — well, business side of things, even if we told her.'

'I wonder! Anyway, love, when does childhood end and young adulthood begin? I can understand her thinking we want to have it both ways — to keep her a child in obedience, and an adult in responsibilities. She shouldn't have been rude and she shouldn't sulk, but I'm afraid she does have some justification.'

44

Good old Mum! I couldn't hear Dad's answer, because just then one of the cats yelled to go into the room and I didn't want them to open the door and find me there, listening. So I spoke to the cat, opened the door myself and went in. I didn't allow any time for uncomfortable moments, but said straight away:

'Sorry I was rude – but now, I've got a proposition to make to save arguments in the future. I want to invest fifty pounds as a shareholder in Tremayne's Nurseries. Plus a set amount of working time. I want to know exactly what I'm expected to do and have specific areas of responsibility. Dad, you worried about Paul and Steve and their days off – I reckon you, Mum and me ought also to have set days off when we know we're free to do whatever we like and can make arrangements accordingly. I'm ready to be flexible to meet emergency requirements, but I think we should establish a proper working relationship.'

I'd lifted a lot of that statement from bits I'd read in papers, or learned in the broad Social and Commerce course I'd opted for at my old school – and it certainly sounded impressive! Dad looked faintly shell-shocked and Mum smiled wickedly at him.

'Hear, hear!' she said.

They were sitting together on the sofa so I went over and sat on the carpet, in front of them. 'I'm truly sorry I said such awful things,' I continued. 'I'll try not to be like that again, honest – I don't know what's got into me, I've been up and down like a yoyo ever since we moved. I think I'll be better when we've settled in a bit, it's just . . .'

'It's just a lot of changes to take in all at once and we've been wrong expecting you to sail through serenely,' Mum said gently, glancing at Dad. 'Perhaps we've been a bit too tied up in our side of things to really think how you're feeling. It's a difficult time for all of us, and we're all going to have to make allowances.'

Then Dad made a very big admission, and the last of my anger vanished. 'I think I've been more upset at leaving Peveran – and my shop – than I would admit even to myself. Perhaps I haven't been thinking quite straight so far as you were concerned. You don't need to put your fifty pounds in to help us out – we're not that desperate. But if you would really like to be a partner, I for one would be glad to have you – and I'm sure your Grandad would, too.'

'I want to be a partner,' I confirmed. 'Really. Maybe we could help Steve be more involved too; with us all pulling like mad for Tremayne's nurseries, we'd just have to succeed!'

We all shook hands on it, then I kissed them goodnight and went up to bed again, only much more happily this time. It was good to think that I could wake up to a friendly morning, with everything back to being right. And maybe, just maybe, I really was starting to grow up . . . and they knew it.

Exhausted (it was now almost midnight) but content, I nudged the cats to one side, crawled into bed, and fell asleep in seconds.

CHAPTER 4

DO MIRACLES HAPPEN?

Mum woke me at eight the next morning. I gulped down my breakfast, then hurried across to tell Celia I couldn't go swimming, and why. I didn't moan about it, and she wasn't in the least bit peeved.

'Tell you what,' she said, 'swimming on your own isn't much fun – shall I come over and help you with the wreaths? And maybe you could help me babysit for the Terrible Twins on Friday when Mum goes out?'

'Sure,' I grinned. 'If we each tie one up, they ought to behave themselves.'

So Celia came over, and with her help I was able to do the wreaths in record time, plus a few extra in case we had more orders. As we worked, we chatted, and guess what the main subject was? Ballet! I didn't mind, though. Because I've never done it myself, or even seen any except on the telly, I was quite interested. It was a bit of a giggle too – in the middle of passing me some holly, Celia would suddenly demonstrate an arabesque, or she'd use the table top as a barre to show me some of the exercises she did morning and evening. It sounded too much like hard work to me! But apparently if you wanted to be a good dancer, you had to practise for hours, until it hurt. She'd done some exams and could go on her points but she said most girls her age were more advanced.

'I don't suppose I ever will be a classical ballerina,' she admitted. 'But there are other kinds of dancing. I'd like to join one of the modern mime-dance companies, and do a lot of choreography. That's what I like most of all, seeing a dance in my mind then making it real. The one I did yesterday was all right, wasn't it?'

I reassured her it was great.

'You can use dance to say a lot of things. Have you ever seen Wayne Sleep?'

I hadn't — which in Celia's view was ten times worse than not knowing who was top of the charts! So I got told about Wayne Sleep and half a dozen other dancers, until for the first time I began to feel a bit of sympathy for Mike — Celia certainly went on a bit when she got half a chance!

But then I persuaded Celia to dance different people, which was much more fun. And watching her, I began to get another of my brilliant ideas. Paul wanted to say things with his music; Celia wanted to say things with her dancing, and they both needed to be Discovered. If Paul really could get his rock opera together and it was as good as I thought it would be, and Celia could do a dance that was part of it, and it could be performed somewhere that important people would go to . . .

But I didn't say anything to her, not then. It was too early. I think Paul's uncertainty about his 'masterpiece' had affected me and of course I'd only heard bits. It was not until later that I was *sure*.

The next day I had a nice surprise. When I was having breakfast, Dad said, 'Shake the mothballs out of your swimsuit — you worked so hard yesterday, you're due for a reward, and so's your Mum. I'm giving you both the morning off.'

'I'm going into Aylesbury, Christmas shopping,' Mum explained. 'I thought you and Celia and maybe the two girls from the farm just up the road might like to go swimming while I go round the shops.'

48

Wouldn't we just! So I went straight over to Celia — she was able to come, and she knew the two girls, Kate and Jenny.

'They're the ones I mentioned — they're nice but they go to boarding school, so I only see them in the holidays,' she said, and suggested we phoned them from her place. They were glad to come, and asked us if we'd like to come back afterwards and ride their horses.

Now as I know from painful experience that if a horse goes any faster than a trot, I fall off, I didn't exactly bounce up and down with excitement at *that* idea, but Celia put her hand over the mouthpiece of the phone and whispered, 'They're very old, slow horses!' so I grinned and nodded.

'Say thanks and yes, then,' I whispered back. 'But only if I'm not needed at the nurseries when we get back.' I'd learned my lesson!

As it happened, I wasn't needed, so we had a super day — nearly all the morning in the swimming pool and it wasn't very busy so we could really have fun. Then up at Kate and Jenny's farm during the afternoon, plodding round on a couple of fat, retired horses. Altogether, the Draysons had six horses and one donkey — apart from Kate's own young hunter, which she was training for show work, they were all waifs and strays.

'This one's owner went to University and asked us to board the mare for her, but then she went to live in Greece and the mare just stayed,' Jenny explained, stroking her own mount. 'And the two geldings you are riding came to us via the RSPCA when this absolutely awful riding school was closed down and its owner prosecuted. The donkey had two horrible child owners, so sensibly he bit them, and Mum just rescued him from the knacker's in time. We've one other mare who's on her last legs now but at least she had three extra years of comfortable living with us.'

Their farm was a bit unusual in that they just ran a small flock of rare Jacob's sheep, but apart from that it was a nice, typical, farmy farm, all muck and wellies, a few hunting cats who lived mainly in the barns and two friendly spaniels who stayed with us all afternoon. When we left, Kate and Jenny invited us, plus Mike and Peter, up on Boxing Day.

'If it snows,' Kate explained, 'we have a sledging party. If it freezes, a sliding and skating party. If it does nothing in particular or just rains, we have any kind of party we think of on the day.'

'I'd love to come, but I've got a disabled friend staying that day,' I said. 'Her name's Stella – could I bring her too?'

'Sure – the more the merrier!'

'And a friend of mine might come down,' Celia added, and I'll swear she blushed. 'Could he come?'

'Boyfriend?' Kate asked curiously, and this time she *definitely* blushed!

'Just a friend.'

'Great – bring him along.'

Of course, as we walked home from the Draysons, I was dying to ask Celia who the boy was, but I didn't want to be nosey or tease her. So I kept heroically quiet for at least two hundred yards, then just as I was beginning to think I must ask or bust, she said, 'The boy who might be coming – he's not a boyfriend exactly, though he's ever so nice. He's the brother of one of the men who flies with the club, and his name's David. He's sixteen. Charles, his brother, has booked a plane for Boxing Day – it's kind of traditional then for club members to fly and have a special lunch – and I'm hoping he'll bring Dave with him.'

'Hope he comes, for your sake. And I promise I won't poach or tease you.'

It did make me feel a bit jealous though. I didn't want a Mad Romance, and I suppose it was awfully fickle when I'd only said goodbye to Andy a few days before, but . . . well, it *is* nice to have boyfriends as well as girlfriends. Especially if you're a bit of a tomboy like me. I wanted someone who would like me, think I was nice and special even if I wasn't pretty. But I couldn't see either Mike or his friend Peter qualifying!

On Friday, as I'd promised, I helped Celia look after the twins. The secretary of the flying school had finished for the Christmas holidays but the school hadn't, so Mrs Burnett was looking after the office.

Running a flying school must be quite complicated really. Students have to be booked in and out; you have to man a control tower and keep a check on the weather; you need to know who's supposed to be turning up and when (and what to do if they don't arrive – after all, they could have crashed somewhere). The planes have to be maintained and fuelled, and the Burnetts also ran a café for the pilots. (Well, they paid two women from the village to run it.)

I liked the planes; they were just two- and four-seaters, small and friendly. There were gliders, too – I could see Mike, all afternoon, holding wingtips and signalling to the tow pilot. But Celia and I kept the twins in for a bit – we made mince pies and let them play with balls of pastry. It's as good as modelling clay and we cooked the results! Then we took them to play in the snow in fields behind the airfield.

Did you know little kids talk all the time? Well, they do! Celia and I could hardly manage to say a sentence without one of them butting in.

'Father Christmas is going to bring me a dolly!'

'I want a nose for my snowman.'

51

'When will it be Christmas?'

'Next time,' I said to Celia, after the 957th interruption, 'I'm going to make some stickjaw toffee. Maybe that'll shut them up!'

She just grinned — she was used to them, and pretty good with them, really. But I must admit I was secretly glad I didn't have any little brothers and sisters, and I could understand why Mike preferred to spend his time helping with the gliders!

I would have liked to go across and ask if I could help too — it looked fun — but I'd promised to help Celia, and anyway I wasn't sure how Mike would welcome me. We didn't seem exactly born to be best friends. So I just stayed with Celia till her Mum came back, then went home and collapsed into a chair with a book. You won't catch me marrying young and immediately having kids — the twins had worn me out in just one afternoon and I didn't somehow think I was really the maternal type!

Next day was Christmas Eve. The hospital visiting times had been relaxed, so Mum took me to see Grandad in the morning. The ward was very empty because all those who could be allowed home had gone but it was cheerful, and bright with decorations. Grandad assured me that patients in hospital at Christmas got spoiled, and he was quite looking forward to it. They'd already had a panto performed by some of the staff and tonight the nurses would come round carol singing. He advised me, though, to go to the Midnight Service in the village church.

'It's beautiful,' he assured me, 'and really starts Christmas off on the right foot.'

But though I considered going, I sold Christmas trees all afternoon to last-minute customers and I knew I'd be half asleep by evening. Anyway, if I went to bed early, Mum could go with Dad, then she could lie in on Christmas morning while I got up at 6 a.m. to put the turkey on. And if that sounds noble, I'd better explain that I always wake early on Christmas Day, eager to see what I've got in the way of pressies, and I could go back to bed and gloat over them the minute the turkey was in the oven!

In the afternoon it was cold and when Celia came across briefly she said she hoped it would freeze hard until Boxing Day, because Dave was training to be a skater. (He did ballet classes to help with his freestyle skating. It counted a lot to her but made Mike write him off as effeminate – typical Mike. I even considered giving him a Male Chauvinist Pig tie for Christmas, but while being rude in fun to friends is all right, I couldn't really be rude to someone I hardly knew and didn't like much!)

I didn't really want frost – I wanted snow, and a real White Christmas, so I watched the sky hopefully all afternoon!

We shut early and Dad took Steve hospital visiting. They'd only just got back when we had a super surprise – a phone call from Peveran vicarage, with all our friends in Cornwall taking turns to speak to us! We'd left presents with everyone before we moved, telling them not to open them until Christmas Day, but Serena obviously hadn't been able to resist temptation, because she thanked me for the Beauty Set I'd given her. And as I'd already opened *her* present, I could hardly tell her off!

Then we settled in for the evening. We all felt uncomfortable at the idea of Paul alone in his bedsit on Christmas Eve so we persuaded him to join us and to play and sing some of his rock opera for Mum and Dad. By then he'd got more of it together and accompanied himself on his guitar. And Mum, who can sight-read really well, sang some of the female bits. My Mum, belting out rock! I'd have curled up laughing, except it sounded quite good.

It's hard to explain, but the more I listened, the

more I became convinced that the music and the words were *right*. Paul might be afraid the world would be blown to bits, but he wasn't resigned to it, and it showed in his music. He was determined we would make peace work somehow – our generation, I mean. It was fierce and exciting, and . . .

Well, have you ever had the feeling that something is good and beautiful and simply has to happen? Even against all the odds, like Dr Barnardo and his Homes and Mother Teresa, things like that. Or Flip going off to Dunkirk in that book, *The Snow Goose*. I had this funny feeling that though the music and the words were Paul's, God had given him the ideas in the first place. Everything he sang was aimed towards getting rid of selfishness, cruelty, prejudice and war, with everyone learning to live together in one peaceful world. And you can't get more right than that, can you?

'It's great and it's *got* to be performed,' I almost yelled when Paul had finished.

Dad agreed. 'I gather they have a Music Festival at Whitsun, at the Conference Centre near here – why not approach them?' he suggested.

'I'm afraid they wouldn't touch it with a bargepole, Mr Tremayne,' Paul answered, smiling wryly. 'Mrs de Lacey, who is a battleaxe of the first order, has made that Festival one of the most respected in the English music world, in just a few years. They have top professional performers, and her organizing committee is full of the most important people going. *They* might look at a work by an unknown, but Mrs de Lacey wouldn't. The festival is one of her big charity efforts, all profits to Dr Barnardo's and National Children's Homes, and her target is high. To get people to pay her kind of ticket prices, she knows she has to have famous names – I'm afraid a bunch of students just wouldn't qualify. Anyway, I need a very special tenor and

54

soprano for the leading roles.'

He paused, shrugged and smiled. 'But you must be getting bored with me and my music.'

'Not at all,' Mum said, and it was true. We were all really interested.

'So what is the particular problem regarding the tenor and soprano?' Dad asked.

'They have to have the range and training for opera, but be able to sing rock. I don't know any students who can do it and most of them wouldn't even be allowed to try. Singing teachers are very strict about what their students are allowed to attempt.'

He paused again, then produced his final obstacle. 'And I haven't got any money. I couldn't pay anyone expenses, let alone fees, or hire halls for rehearsals, performances, anything.'

'Defeatist!' I muttered, and Mum said something about how he could apply to the Arts Council or someone like that for a grant. Then I said something which took even *me* by surprise – it just came out.

'If God wants your rock opera to be performed – and I reckon he gave you the music and the words, sort of commissioned it whether you know it or not – then he'll provide everything you need to have it performed,' I pronounced confidently. Even Mum and Dad looked startled – poor old Paul certainly did!

'Hey, what gives you that idea?' he demanded. 'I'm not even on his side, let alone his payroll!'

'You may not be a signed on the dotted line Christian, but you and your music are working for peace,' I replied, 'and that's always OK by God. Blessed are the Peacemakers, remember, for they shall be called the Children of God?'

Then I flushed, realizing I was preaching at him, and apologized; but he seemed more amused than annoyed.

'I'd like to see it come off,' he admitted. 'Not just because I wrote it, but because I believe peace needs all the help it can get, or maybe we won't have a world soon. You can pray for it if you like, Fran – that's your scene. But don't be too hurt if nothing happens. Frankly, I don't believe in miracles.'

Fair enough. That night, I prayed for Paul's rock opera to be performed and for Paul himself. It was rather a vague prayer because I didn't know enough about him, so I asked that whatever the hassle was between him and his parents, it could be sorted out, and that he'd get to know Jesus like I was getting to know him. It wasn't that I felt superior to him because I was a Christian, or reckoned he *ought* to be one, it's just that if you've got something good, you want to share it!

And I admit I ended up by praying for me – that I could get over being homesick for Peveran and really be happy here. After all, Christmas seemed a particularly right time to pray for miracles!

CHAPTER 5

CHRISTMAS AT THE NURSERIES

Christmas Day dawned bright and snow-free. I got up early as planned, put the turkey in and fed the cats (who howled because they wanted turkey not something out of a tin but I told them they'd have to wait). Then I returned to bed and opened my little presents – the big ones we always saved to open after lunch. But even the little pressies were super – best of all, a pack of ten shorthand notebooks and biros from Mum and Dad. I'm always practising writing so I get through loads of paper. Paul had given me a record by my favourite group, which I thought was really nice as he'd only known me such a short while and Steve had left me a book on flowers. All I'd managed for them were long furry snake draught excluders – I gave Paul his before he borrowed the van and went off to spend the day with his parents.

There was a short service at church in the morning, and I met up with Jenny and Kate and we exchanged cards – ditto Mike and Peter. Celia and I had presents for each other. I gave her a ballet picture, and she gave me a cat picture. After church, we whipped into hospital to give Grandad his presents. He must have got one of the nurses to go shopping for him because he had ours as well. Mine was a second-hand pair of skating boots! When we left, the food trolleys were arriving and it was obvious by the smell that there was going to be a full scale traditional Christmas dinner for everyone. I'd been starving before but, what with that smell, by the time we got home I was absolutely ravenous!

When we did get down to eating, we all had far too much – as usual – and sprawled, feeling bloated, to open our presents and listen to the Queen's Speech.

At about 3.30 I decided I must walk off some of the turkey and pud, and went across to the airfield to see if Celia fancied a walk. She did, and we meandered along the river bank, all the way to the convent and back. Part way back we met Jenny and Kate, out riding, with the dogs. Kate looked up at the leaden sky. 'It'll snow in the night,' she pronounced.

'Hope it snows lots,' Jenny agreed.

'But not enough to close the roads,' I warned, because we had to fetch Stella and I didn't want her day spoiled.

'Nor to stop flying!' Celia said and I knew she was thinking Dave couldn't come if his brother didn't come down to fly!

Luckily, the weather must have listened to us more than to Kate and Jenny because, though it did snow a bit in the evening, Boxing Day morning was clear, and Dad had no problems driving up for Stella. Stella is completely paralysed and has to spend her time in a wheelchair. When she'd come down to Peveran in Cornwall she'd been living in the long-stay ward of a children's hospital, but since then she and two of the other kids who'd come down with her had been placed in proper residential homes for the disabled. Stella's home was attached to a school that she liked a lot, where she could actually do O-level art (she mouthpaints) and it was only a couple of hours' drive away from where we now lived. I wondered if it was the letters from my dad and Mr McKay and the Kerseys which had woken the social workers up a bit and got her moved! When we arrived she was in her outdoor gear, ready, eager and excited. I felt a bit guilty because we couldn't take any of the others with us, but she was my special friend and anyway she said they had lots of things happening over Christmas.

I could hardly wait to get Stella home, to see the special presents we'd got waiting for her. Before I'd left Peveran I'd done a sponsored sing, just me with Mrs McKay on the piano and I'd bullied most of the village and my friends at school into sponsoring me. I'd raised over fifty pounds and had got a combined easel and tray that fitted on Stella's wheelchair. Because she couldn't move to look round the easel, it had an electronically operated hinge so at the push of a button (operated by her mouthstick) it would swivel out of the way to let her study whatever she was painting. It had been specially made by a friend of ours who was an engineer, and though he'd spent hours on it, he'd only charged for materials.

Then Mum and Dad and a few other friends had pooled together to buy something else to help her artistic career – an ordinary camera, which would fit on the wheelchair at the right height for her to use the viewfinder, and operate it with her mouthstick. So, if she couldn't paint a scene live, she could photograph it and paint it later from the photo.

She was thrilled to bits! And it was all worth it – you'd believe me if you could see the pictures she'd painted for our presents. I wasn't just kidding myself they were good because I felt sorry for her for being disabled. I'd have thought they were good if I hadn't known who'd painted them, or that they'd been done with a brush held between her teeth. (In fact I proved it later by putting a flower one on show in the Nurseries' shop, and a customer admired it and wanted to buy it.)

We hadn't arrived home until just before lunch, so we didn't go out again until mid-afternoon. Because it looked as if it was going to snow again, Mum and Dad said they'd visit Grandad and then they wanted to take Stella back at about 4 p.m. Although this meant we could only have a very brief stay at Kate and Jenny's, we both fancied going, so I started to push Stella up the road. Paul saw and offered to help. I was glad to accept because the last bit of lane up to the farm was pretty rough. I didn't like to ask how his day with his parents had gone, just in case it had been awful! He was very nice to Stella and so, surprisingly enough, was Mike. I suppose it helped that she was interested in the planes flying from his dad's club and wanted to photograph them, so he was able to show off his knowledge and she was duly impressed.

Stella has this way of being sweet and feminine, which boys seem to like and which I'm absolutely no good at! So Mike and Paul chatted to Stella and Celia chatted to me (when she wasn't looking down the road hoping to see David coming) and Kate and Jenny gave us hot mince pies and chestnuts and decided to set up a treasure hunt as there wasn't enough snow for sledging or ice for skating. Peter turned up with a giggling, blonde who struck me as having a large size in bras and a small size in brain, though she was nice enough; and about fifteen minutes after we'd arrived, a dark boy came racing along. When I saw happiness flood Celia's face I knew Dreamboat Dave had joined the party.

'David!' Celia exclaimed happily. 'I thought you and Charles weren't coming after all.'

'There was an accident blocking the road and we had to divert round miles of windy, slippery lanes,' the boy panted. 'Sorry I'm late, happy Christmas – your pressie's back at the field, I just asked your Dad the way here then ran up. These are for Kate and Jenny.'

He held out a box of chocolates and Kate and Jenny at once did the polite hostess bit, saying how kind and oh, you shouldn't have . . . so the rest of us promptly said that if they felt guilty at accepting the chocs, we'd eat them. We ended up all having some and I prodded my middle to see if there was a spare tyre starting yet! Then Kate and Jenny vanished to set the clues, but by then we already had to head for home. Paul helped me with the pushing back, chatting to Stella as if he'd known her for years. Perhaps it was because they were both creative – they just seemed to get on naturally. And they had common ground, because she lived near some friends of his. Paul often visited them for the weekend when he was studying up in London.

'Do you reckon the staff would let a disreputable music student take you out from time to time? Purely platonic, of course.'

Stella made a face at the 'platonic', just for fun. Paul was too old for her really. But she wasn't going to turn down any chance of getting out into the big bad world, away from the Home and School.

'If you came back with me this evening,' she said hopefully, 'and Fran's mum established you as a Responsible Person, I think they might. They have to be a bit choosy about who we go out with, because I suppose they'd be blamed if anything went wrong – but they're not stuffy about it.'

'I shall wear a hat and my most respectable, clean clothes,' Paul promised. 'I shall behave in a sober and proper manner, and give my Boy Scout's honour to look after you properly. Anyway, it would only be to perfectly proper things. It's just that as a music student I sometimes get free or very cheap tickets to hear some really good music, and I also like to go up to the big London galleries – we can get in cheap there, too. Music's my first love, but art is my second.'

I don't think he realized he'd practically offered her heaven on a plate! I did, though, and I was really glad for her. So we decided that Dad would drive Stella back and Paul would go with them to be introduced. Mum was going anyway because she wanted to ask the Matron what special provisions she would need to make (apart from a bed downstairs) if we were to have Stella to stay overnight.

The only slight problem was that there was no room left in the car for me. And while I reckoned I was quite old enough to be left alone, Mum obviously had visions of the countryside being full of villains and murderers, so she insisted I should go over to the Burnetts for the evening. Honestly! Not that they minded (she rang Mrs Burnett up) but anyone would think I was a little kid in need of a baby-sitter! Trouble is, when Mum gets one of her worry moods nothing convinces her and though I was fuming I reminded myself it was Christmas and I wasn't going to spoil the day by arguing. So I dutifully trudged over to the airfield as soon as I'd waved goodbye to Stella.

The airfield was just a peaceful crisscross of snow and cleared runways, but I wondered what it had been like in the war, when it was used for training fighter pilots. Had Spitfires zoomed over our house? Maybe a girl watched them, dreading the day when her pilot would have to go to another base where he and his plane would be hurled at wave after wave of enemy Messerschmidts? It sounded romantic but ended up with people being killed. And if we had a world war now, it wouldn't be romantic at all, just people wiped out in millions. Paul was right about us needing peace; it was OK to be romantic about courage, but not about war. I suppose, deep down, that I wasn't 100 per cent pacifist. I couldn't put up with being ruled by someone like Hitler, couldn't allow cruelty and injustice. I would fight for a better world, but there just had to be ways of fighting without killing. Peace Corps people had to be just as brave as soldiers. Perhaps when

I was old enough and had some kind of useful skill to offer, I could do something, go out to the Third World? For a moment I almost wished I could fly — I could be a pilot for Flying Doctor. But I still had the horrible feeling that the very first lesson, I'd land on our house or something stupid. At least with sailing, the worst you can do is capsize! So I shook off my daydreams and ran the last few yards to the Burnetts.

The twins, thank goodness, had been tired out from trying to break all their presents and stuffing themselves with food, so they'd gone to bed. But David was still there (looking romantically at Celia) and there was also the most dishy man I have *ever* seen, who turned out to be Charles, David's big brother. He was the one who flew. Mike was there too, but very quiet. Charles had given him a big, glossy flying book for Christmas. Apart from the occasional 'Wow!' and 'Wouldn't I like to fly *you*', he didn't contribute much to the conversation. Mr Burnett and Charles were talking flying. Charles had got his private pilot's licence but was talking about going on to take different 'ratings' so he could fly on instruments and at night. He also fancied learning to fly helicopters but Mr Burnett didn't do that because they're very expensive to run. It costs about a thousand pounds just to learn to fly an ordinary plane, so I don't think I ever will be a pilot anyway! Mrs Burnett half joined in the conversation, while I just tried to look politely interested, wishing Mum had let me stay in our house, where at least I could have watched Disneytime on the telly!

It was Charles McLaren who saved me. He didn't actually say, 'Poor Fran's bored out of her mind' but he gave me a sympathetic look and suggested we played Monopoly or something.

'No, let's have a singsong,' Mrs Burnett responded

quickly. (I think she'd been bored, too.) 'We haven't heard you for ages, Charles.'

'OK. But everyone's got to join in.'

That was fine by me. I've got a passable voice, in a folksy sort of way. Even Mike was dragged out of his book and came to lean on the piano. Charles played, by ear, picking out the tunes as they were requested. Mike, of course, had to begin with that gory parachute one — 'He jumped from 20,000 feet without a parachute . . .', while Mrs Burnett liked songs from musicals and Mr Burnett liked the naughtier kind of folk songs! Celia wanted pop. (Well, you can't sing ballet music, or I'm sure she would have had Swan Lake.) Dave was keen on opera. At first, I just warbled along happily with them — then after a bit, something rather important began to sink into my brain. The Burnetts were used to having singsongs and they obviously had them mainly because they liked listening to Charles. It was a cheating way of getting him to do a recital!

Because Charles had A Voice. Not content with looking tall, dark and gorgeous, he had a fantastic tenor voice. It didn't show to much advantage in Clementine but when Dave asked for the Toreador Song — wow!

The little cogs in my brain started to slip into place and I asked him to sing a real rock number that was climbing the charts fast. He knew it, he sang it, and it sounded great! When he'd finished I clapped so enthusiastically he looked surprised as well as pleased. Later, when we'd stopped singing and were having hot chocolate, I told him why I'd got so excited because he could sing both opera and rock. Thank goodness, he was interested, really keen to see the music for Paul's rock opera.

'Trouble is, we'll have to be leaving soon — probably before your friend Paul gets back,' he said.

Luckily, that didn't matter. I remembered Paul had left

most of his rough score in our sitting-room after he'd played it to us on Christmas Eve. I was sure he wouldn't mind me showing Charles — and I had a key.

'Would you — could you come over now?' I urged, and after a word of explanation to Mrs Burnett, he agreed.

It was as simple as that. Charles came over with me, leafed through Paul's score, playing and singing little bits here and there, and decided he liked it a lot.

'It is difficult,' he agreed after a while, 'but it's fascinating. Tenors usually get stuck with being the hero. It's a real challenge for the tenor to be the baddy. And Mr Hawk has to sing his way through so many musical moods. Here, he's the Establishment — here, he's fierce, a killer — here, he's very sly, persuasive. Yes, I'd love to sing this . . . and yes, Fran, you're dead right. This *is* good music and important words, it ought to be performed. If your friend Paul would like me to sing it, I'd be delighted to have a go.'

'Paul hasn't quite finished it yet,' I admitted. 'And he hasn't got any idea where it can be performed. In fact he's a bit of a defeatist because he reckons nobody will want to put on work by students and unknowns. But I'm sure it will come off, somehow! Would it be OK if I asked him to let you have a photocopy of the score, so you can learn it, then actually work on it with everyone else if and when they start rehearsing for an actual performance?'

'Fine by me,' he agreed. 'But look, I could come down again tomorrow, and have a word with Paul about it. That might be best. After all, he might not think I suit the role.'

I was sure he would, but to be on the safe side I suggested Charles came down in the morning, saw Paul and stayed to lunch. David could come too if he liked (well, I had to do my bit for Celia's romance, didn't I?). So that was agreed and we walked back to the Burnetts because it was time for him and Dave to go. But as they went, he said

65

something that really made my day.

'The forecast is rather poor tomorrow for flying, but would you like it if I asked your parents' permission to take you the next time I go up?'

Would I? Well, honestly — who wouldn't?

'You bet! I'd love to!' I breathed.

When Mum and Dad got back with Paul and Mum came to collect me from the Burnetts, I was absolutely walking on air and couldn't wait to ask her if I could fly with Charles. But she wouldn't give me a definite answer until she'd asked Dad. When she did, he wanted to wait until they'd both met him.

'He'll be down tomorrow to see Paul about his music — I hope you don't mind, I've invited him to lunch,' I said eagerly. They didn't mind at all, but Mum was a bit puzzled.

'Why is he interested in Paul's music?' she asked, so I told her — and Paul who'd joined us by then — that I thought Charles was just the person he needed for his male lead. Paul just grinned and looked at me sideways. Somehow I think he doubted my musical judgement!

'He really is good,' I assured him. 'He came over and had a go at it, and is really keen to sing it, if you'll let him. He's ever so nice, I shouldn't think he's much older than you. I don't think he's a music student; I suppose he's just an amateur but he really has got a super voice and he can play the piano by ear too. His name's Charles McLaren.'

Paul's expression changed to astonishment and he stared at me. 'Charles McLaren has been here, looked at my score and wants it?' he asked unbelievingly. 'Do you know who he is?'

He said it in the tone of voice people use when speaking of someone incredibly important, so it was my turn to be bewildered.

66

'Charles McLaren is the Boy Wonder of English opera. The critics rave about him because he has the right looks for a romantic tenor, plus a voice of magnificent control, accuracy, power and feeling. I quote. He's just landed a real plum job making a series of "location" operas for television. And the incredible thing is, he shouldn't be an opera singer at all because by all the rules he should have wrecked his voice as a kid, when he sang in a little tinpot group with some of his friends. If I'd daydreamed, I might have chosen him for Mr Hawk — but I just can't believe you've produced him out of a hat!'

Mum grinned. 'Looks like Fran is right, and God does want your rock opera performed,' she said.

Poor old Paul was too flattened to argue. 'And he liked it? He actually wants to sing it?'

'He thinks the words and music are great,' I confirmed. 'But are you sure my Charles McLaren is the same one? He doesn't *act* important and famous, he's just nice and normal.'

'What does he look like?'

'Dishy!' I breathed and Mum laughed.

'He could be the same one,' Dad said. 'After all, not all famous people let it go to their heads. He may just be a very sensible and down-to-earth young man.'

'In which case you'll let me fly with him? Mr Burnett taught him, he has got a licence . . .'

'We'll see,' was all Dad would say. Then he announced that he, for one, was starving hungry, so I made sandwiches for them all with left-over turkey and Boxing Day ham. I didn't eat any because I'd stuffed myself at the Burnetts and was beginning to think I would weigh at least eighteen stone if I kept up that kind of eating until the New Year! Mind you, Paul barely touched his sandwiches. He was too excited to eat and just in case my Charles McLaren was *the* one, he wanted to get back to his bedsit and start writing the last bit of music. I was pretty excited myself — now all we needed was somewhere to perform and a very special soprano. All in all, it had been a great day!

CHAPTER 6

THE LADY OF THE MANOR

I had a feeling that things were getting better and better.
And I was right, too. First of all, I woke up to lots of snow.
Then at 9.30 Jenny rang to invite me to go sledging on
their sloping field. They'd already rung Celia but she was
going to hang around the airfield in the hopes that the
roads would be clear enough for Charles to come (and bring
David), then they'd come up together. I did a bit of snow
clearing for Mum, then shot off to the farm.

Charles and David did make it, and when Celia and
David joined us, I asked him if his brother was a famous
opera singer. He grinned. 'I suppose he is, but he gets
embarrassed about it,' he admitted. 'It's dead funny, really.
Since he appeared on telly in *Tristan and Isolde*, women
have started sending him romantic fan letters!'

I didn't blame them one bit – in fact, once I knew he'd
come, I stopped sledging, making the excuse that I had
to get back to help Mum with the lunch. But really I
wanted to hang around while Charles was there! To begin
with, though, he was in with Paul, the guitar going full
blast and him singing. We could hear them clearly from
the kitchen, and Mum was listening with a dreamy
expression on her face.

'What a glorious voice!' she said. 'And what a very nice
young man.'

'So you'll let him take me flying?'

'Maybe . . .'

But I wouldn't let her escape. As we talked over lunch, I could see Mum and Dad were really impressed with Charles as a person, though that didn't necessarily mean they would trust him as a pilot. So I steered the conversation towards his flying experience, got him to talk about all the things you had to do when you were learning and how hard it was to pass your licence – so they would know he had to be good and able to cope with any emergency. After that, I got him on to safety standards and statistics (trying like mad to convince them I'd be safer in a plane than in a car) and eventually I got them to agree that it would be OK for me to go up with Charles, providing the weather was suitable. But Mum made him promise to take me for a brief flight only, with absolutely no stunts! Charles said he'd give us a ring as soon as he had a free day at a weekend and the weather was right – then I had to say goodbye because I was going with Mum to visit Grandad.

Grandad was full of the joys of spring because he'd been helped out of bed and into a chair for the first time, which had made him feel a bit peculiar and dizzy at first, but it was a big step towards getting better and coming home.

'Be running down the ward before you know it!' he chuckled.

Then he and Mum talked about his plans for when he came out, though that would be quite a way in the future. Arrangements were already in hand for some adaptations that would allow him to be as independent as possible. Although he could probably just about manage stairs, his left leg and arm were weakened and he'd decided a ground-floor flat would be the best in the long term. Part of the upstairs of his house had already been turned into a bedsit (where Paul lived) and he reckoned it would be sensible to convert the other rooms into a flat. It would have one bedroom, a lounge-diner and kitchenette, plus the bathroom and loo that were already up there. His idea was that when Steve got married, he might like to live there. That meant another toilet and bathroom would have to be added downstairs.

'Reckon that'll suit me nicely – big enough to have visitors, but not too big to look after,' Grandad said. Then he went on to warn us that we could expect business at the Nurseries to be dead for a while. There would be work to do, but not much money to take. 'We could do with some kind of regular contract work, to tide us over the slack times,' he said. But when we left the hospital he was in fine form, joking with the nurses.

When Mum and I reported back to Dad and Paul what Grandad said about business, they agreed. Dad had been looking through the previous year's books and he said that from Christmas to the end of January, the takings were very low indeed.

'It's a great pity we can't get something from the Manor,' Dad said. 'Even apart from what they must need to put into the gardens each year, a big Conference Centre like that is bound to have a demand for house plants.'

'Why don't we go up there, introduce ourselves, and do a hard sell?' I suggested, but Dad didn't think that was the right approach. To be honest, he just isn't the pushy type, and nor is Mum.

However, there's a saying that if Muhammad won't go to the mountain, the mountain must come to Muhammad. I wouldn't exactly call Mrs de Lacey of the Manor a mountain (a Sherman tank, maybe) but she was certainly a big, forceful lady and she came to us on New Year's Eve at 5.35 p.m. I know the exact time because we'd hardly had a customer all day and in the afternoon Mum, Dad and Steve had all gone to see Grandad, leaving Paul and me in charge. I'd told Paul he might just as well go and work on his music while I sat in the office and wrote,

71

because, let's face it, who's going to buy anything in the plant line on New Year's Eve! They'd all be in the towns stocking up on food and drink!

As usual, when I'm writing, I got carried away and it was gone 5.30 when I realized we should have shut, but I hadn't put up the closed sign outside our gate. As I went to do this, I saw the car coming down the road and thought at first it was our mob coming back — but it was a rather classy Peugeot, and it turned in at our gates.

Mrs Adelaide de Lacey was gracing us with her custom! Of course, I didn't have a clue who she was to begin with, but she soon identified herself and demanded to see the person in charge. I said that for the moment it was me (Paul was older, but I was a partner!). That didn't go down very well, but she grudgingly decided I would have to do.

'My usual suppliers have let me down in the most atrocious manner,' she said. (They would doubtless be shot at dawn.) 'I have a charity ball tonight, and must disguise a very rugged and ugly temporary stage. Unfortunately, all the major florists and nurseries are now shut.'

'So are we, as a matter of fact,' I replied calmly. 'But under the circumstances, I am sure we can come to your assistance. What time does the ball start, and what area must we cover?'

'It starts at 7.30 but you must be finished by seven at the latest,' she said, then gave me the dimensions of the stage. It was really only the surface and some unwanted bare steps at the front that we would need to cover.

'Your parents must come up with everything that is necessary the minute they return,' she said.

No way! Mum and Dad were going shopping after visiting, wouldn't be back until after six, and would be both tired and hungry.

'They will not be doing it. I will,' I retorted.

Mrs de Lacey glared at me. 'I cannot imagine you have

sufficient skill or experience,' she said flatly.

I smiled back. 'Frankly, Mrs de Lacey,' I argued, all adult and confident, 'you have no real choice — it's me or nobody. Do you want an ugly, bare stage — or will you trust me to do whatever I can at what is extremely short notice?'

Inwardly, my heart was thumping and I didn't have much clue what I was going to do, but I was blowed if I would let her walk all over me. And if I could only do *something*, it would be money for the Nurseries. I had a vague idea that might work.

'Very well. But your work had better be up to standard, young lady . . .'

With that, she did an about turn and marched off. I ran in search of Paul, and told him what we were going to do.

'But we can't!' he exclaimed. 'I'm no good at that sort of thing, and we haven't got much to decorate a ballroom with . . .'

'Have you seen any of that artificial green grass stuff?' I asked. There had to be some around, I remembered from an autumn holiday that Grandad had stalls out with apples and pears, and this green stuff on them.

'Yes, but it's probably a bit tatty . . .'

'Get all you can lay your hands on, and something for padding — bales of straw would do. I'll pick up some Oasis and a whole lot of heathers, bulbs in pots, primroses, polyanthuses, anything I can find. You get some greenery as well, cut it off our trees. I'll get scissors, nails, hammer, things like that. And I'll ring Celia — we'll need another hand.'

'But what are we going to do?'

'Same sort of thing I once did for a carnival float in Peveran,' I said, and grinned. 'But don't tell Her Ladyship that! To be honest, it's the only thing I have a clue how to do, but I think it'll work.'

73

I didn't dare to think what would happen if it all went wrong; and I told Paul to get a move on so we could be gone before Mum and Dad got back. They might just panic and try to stop us! I rang Celia, but she'd gone into Wycombe with her Mum and hadn't come back. Mike answered the phone and to my astonishment, when I told him why I wanted her, he volunteered to come and help!

'Carrying things,' he said. 'I'm not arranging flowers for anyone!'

Actually, he came in very useful, helping me to get masses of stuff from our greenhouses and sheds and loading it into the van. He thought it was all a hoot, which calmed my nerves a bit – and they did need calming, believe me, when we actually drove into the Manor grounds and I saw what a big, impressive place it was. We parked near a side entrance, unloaded the stuff, and carried it bit by bit into this enormous ballroom. There were some beautiful flower arrangements on pedestals and in one section the most incredible portrait gallery – curtains too, made of a deep red velvet that just breathed money! And right in the middle of all this beauty and luxury was the stage – cobbled together out of any bits of second-hand wood the makers could find, by the look of it.

'We'll need a slight bank of straw round the edge,' I commanded Paul, 'and clumps to break up the outline of the steps.'

Mike helped him. As Paul put the straw down, he anchored it in place with criss-crossed strips of broad sticky tape and plastic sheeting he'd found in the van. I went through the green grass stuff, folding under any really tatty or soiled bits, and then began fixing it across the stage, over the straw heaps and down the steps with a staple gun. We could hear other people, the caterers, working and Mrs de Lacey shouting at them – she tried to shout at us, too, but I was too busy to notice and I half heard Mike calmly

74

telling her to please go away if she wanted us to get on.

'Since when were *you* attached to Tremayne's Nurseries?' she demanded, but she was smiling and he was smiling back at her.

When she'd gone he said cheerfully, 'Don't mind her – the old girl's bark is worse than her bite. Hey, can I have a go with that staple gun?'

'Sure,' I agreed, so he took over fixing the green stuff, while I began to cut flaps in it. I tried putting plants in while still in their pots but it didn't work – they were too high. So I got Paul cutting Oasis into thin circles and soaking it, then I took the plants out of their pots and with a bit of earth clinging to their roots, settled them on the Oasis. Once they were fairly steady, I closed the flaps of green round them as best I could, so they looked as if they were growing in the grass, like plants do in a Cornish hedge. I know it sounds pretty hideous but actually it worked quite well; bits of greenery here and there broke up the unnatural look of the grass stuff, and the ugly stage was suddenly quite a reasonable looking grassy bank with flowers.

Of course, we'd made a lot of mess, bits of earth and green everywhere, but Mrs de Lacey marshalled up three maids who immediately swept and vacuumed, then went over the floor with an electric polisher and some kind of non-slip polish. I looked from the stage to the clock, which said 6.45 p.m.

'Done it!'

'Not bad, not bad at all. Rural simplicity,' Mrs de Lacey acknowledged. 'You are a surprising child. How much do I owe you?'

'We haven't worked it out yet . . .' Paul began.

I cut him short. 'We will only charge you for the plants and Oasis used, plus a small charge to cover the cleaning and repair of the grass fabric. As this is a charity event, we won't charge our labour.'

Mrs de Lacey raised her eyebrows, and half smiled. 'Most generous. Perhaps you will prepare an invoice and let me have it in due course. Now − I cannot tolerate inefficiency, and the excuses of my contract firm for their failure on this occasion do not hold water. On the other hand, I appreciate initiative and efficiency. I shall be calling on Tremayne's Nurseries to discuss contract terms shortly.'

Yippee! We'd won! Somehow, I managed to look and speak calmly, as though it was an everyday event of no particular importance. 'We will look forward to seeing you, and I feel sure we will be able to give you satisfaction in the future.'

Then we left, so the guests who were paying £12 a head for this 'do' wouldn't be confronted by our tatty old van as they arrived in their Rolls Royces.

'I feel sure we will be able to give you every satisfaction in the future,' Mike mimicked, laughing. 'You've got a cheek − but I like it, I like it! Come over and help sell flying lessons some time.'

'After the way you helped tonight,' I said rashly, 'I'll even come over and help you polish planes.'

'I'm reeling,' Paul admitted. 'Do you realize that this means a big chance for the Nurseries? The Manor used to fork out about £100 a *week* to the firm who had the last contract − I remember Steve's dad saying . . .'

I'd promised Mrs de Lacey that we would go up the next day (even though it was New Year's Day and a Bank Holiday) to pick up the grass stuff and straw, and put the plants either in her gardens, or back into pots so they wouldn't be wasted. By now, though, I was beginning to go into shock, realizing what an enormous chance I'd taken, and how horribly wrong everything might have gone! Had it really been me, taking command like that? And Mike, helping? He'd been different − quite nice. I

76

made a mental vow to find some way of thanking him properly. Of course, he liked Grandad and had been to see him a few times since he'd been in hospital, so maybe he'd helped for Grandad's sake, not mine. But he hadn't struck me as the kind who would help at all, and I was beginning to get a guilty feeling that maybe I hadn't given him a fair chance, just because he'd rubbed me up the wrong way the first time we'd met.

'I'll keep you to that offer of helping polish planes,' he threatened as we dropped him off before turning into our gate.

I grinned and said, 'OK. Just give me a yell when you want me.'

Then I went in to explain to Mum and Dad what we'd been up to while they were out. All I'd left was a brief note saying not to worry, we'd gone off on a job for the Nurseries. They were astonished, but very pleased, once they knew everything had worked, and looked right, and that we might even be getting a really good contract.

'Fine work, partner,' Dad approved, and Mum nodded her head.

'Though I don't know how you dared,' she said. 'I've only met Mrs de Lacey once, but the woman absolutely terrified me. I don't know what happened to Mr de Lacey – I imagine she ate him.'

'She's not a bad old bird,' I said with the calmness of hindsight. 'And Mike says her bark is worse than her bite.'

'None the less, we'd better get an invoice ready for her – keep up the good impression. Do you know just what plants you took?'

I did, because I'd got Paul to list them as I was putting them in place.

'I think I'll ring your Grandad and tell him,' Mum said. 'The ward has a phone which can be wheeled to his bedside, and he'll be really pleased to hear what you've done.'

'Tell him Paul and Mike helped.'

'Meanwhile,' Dad said, 'I think this calls for a celebration!'

So we mulled some punch and toasted the Nurseries and the New Year. But I let it come in on its own while I went to bed early − determined to get to the Manor in good time, not just to impress Mrs de Lacey but because now I'd met her, there was a very important question I had to ask.

This time, Dad came with me to the Manor. We cleared the stage together, then he did the repotting and planting while I went in search of Mrs de Lacey. I took the invoice, but that was only an excuse − it was her music festival I wanted to talk about, and Paul's rock opera.

The Ball had gone very well and she was in a really good mood, so she heard me out, and even pricked up her ears at the mention of Charles McLaren. But she told me point-blank that there was no chance of getting Paul's thing into this year's Whitsun Festival.

'All the artistes have been booked for many months,' she assured me. 'However, if you get a score to me, I will ask the committee to consider it for next year.'

'But if someone should drop out, would you consider it for this year?' I urged. I'm not a very patient person!

'Nobody,' she assured me, 'drops out of *my* festival. It is far too good a showcase. But if the impossible should happen, yes, I'll contact you.'

And with that, I had to be content.

CHAPTER 7

BE MY VALENTINE

Over the next few weeks so many things happened that Paul and his music had to take a back seat. Anyway, he went back to his hostel and college early in January and though he wrote and told me he'd got his friends rehearsing, I couldn't feel as involved as if he were still living with us and I could hear the music drifting down from his bedsit.

Celia and I made the most of what was left of the Christmas holidays and the snow to go sledging and skating with Kate and Jenny. After a bit, I started to call Celia just Cee, which I suppose proved we were getting to be real friends! Sometimes Mike and even Peter condescended to join us, and I did keep my promise to help Mike polish an aeroplane (well, three actually). I also went with Celia to her ballet class, just to watch. But though part of me wanted to be able to dance, no way was I going to start doing Positions with little five-year-olds. I really only went to encourage Cee because nobody in her family seemed to care less about ballet.

I had asked Paul to let Celia work out some dancing routines for his rock opera, but he said to leave it until it was definitely on — had somewhere to be performed, anyway — or she might just end up disappointed. So I kept quiet, though it wasn't easy!

Cee kept hoping Dave would come down, and so did I, because if he came, it would be with Charles, and if *he* came it would be to take me flying! It wasn't just the flight I wanted, to be honest – Mr Burnett would have taken me up if I'd asked – it was Charles, too. He was the most absolutely superfantastic, gorgeous man I've ever met and twenty-four isn't that old, is it? I kept telling myself that Dad was seven years older than Mum . . .

But still Charles didn't come and real life intruded in the form of school. The horrible morning came when, all spruced up and in uniform, I set off with Celia for my first day of my first term at the convent, wondering what on earth it would be like. At least the uniform wasn't bad.

Although the convent itself was a beautiful old stone building, the school had been built in the Second World War when the nuns had met an urgent need to accommodate and educate war orphans and evacuees. They had no orphanage now, just the school. After my school in Truro, it seemed tiny – imagine, there were only twenty-four girls in my whole year. We'd had thirty kids in a form and six forms in a year. It felt a bit funny, too, being all girls after having been to mixed schools all my life, but I was relieved to find at least I wasn't behind in any subjects. I'd taken a written exam to get accepted and win the scholarship and in fact I was down to take English with girls in the form above me – they did that kind of cross-age streaming.

There was less mucking about in class than there had been at my old school, but they weren't strict, and all the teachers really liked teaching. The nuns were really good teachers, interested in their subjects and good at making them interesting to us. Some lessons were great. We'd act out the books we read in English and there were lots of projects on the go. And because many of the nuns had done interesting things before coming to the convent, there were lots of optional subjects, to be taken either in Free Periods or after school – craft things in particular.

Cee and I walked to school each day along the river bank

and it helped being her friend already because she introduced me to the other girls and showed me around. She stayed my best friend, though I got on quite well with some of the other girls.

I was also beginning to get friendlier with Mike, especially at weekends because he'd more or less split with Peter and lots of his school friends were boarders who went home on Friday night and didn't get back until Sunday. The trouble with Pete apparently had been that he wanted to spend all his time in coffee bars and discos, chatting up the birds, and though Mike quite likes girls, he likes planes more and he absolutely hates discos! And anyway he prefers the kind of female who is useful, i.e. will hand him tools while he fiddles about with the innards of an old aircraft engine, and I didn't mind doing that sometimes, if I had no jobs at the Nurseries and Cee was off at her ballet class.

But I still woke every Saturday hoping it would be the Saturday that Charles came down. And one glorious day, it was! I was over at the airfield, helping Mike and some of the gliding club members get the gliders out of their hangar, when Mum came running over, flushed and excited.

'Charles McLaren has arrived,' she said. 'He's hiring a four-seater and he asked me if I'd like to go up. He said Dad too, but he's got to go into Wycombe.'

'I'll come if there's a spare seat,' Mike said eagerly. (He never misses any chance.)

'I said I didn't really know – I'm sure I'll be terrified – but he persuaded me,' Mum finished, and I could tell that although she twittered about it like a frightened chick, she was really excited and glad. Like me, she'd never had a chance to fly before.

'You'll love it,' Mike assured her, and I thought how clever Charles was to invite her. Because of course, if she tried it and liked it, and saw for herself how safe it was, she'd not worry if I got the chance to go flying again.

'We're to meet him over on the parking lot.' I knew she didn't mean the car park, but 'Dispersal', the bit of tarmac where the planes wait as pilots go through their pre-flight checks. So we went over, and there was Charles checking out his aircraft. He explained what he was doing – looking at all the moving parts, the tyres, the fuel cap (he'd already checked her for fuel and oil). Then we got in and he offered Mum the front passenger seat, while Mike and I got in the back.

'Right. What do I have to check now?' he asked, and Mike rattled things off. I can't remember them all, but one was fuel, one was full and free movement of controls – there are things called elevators and ailerons that control the up and down and sideways movement of the plane, and flaps that act as a kind of brake in the air. He had to check the compass and the altimeter setting. And he had to run the engine at high revs and at low revs to make sure it worked properly on both. There may have been other things too – it was detailed and thorough, and obviously impressed Mum that Charles was putting safety first. Mike impressed me – he really did know his stuff about flying, even Charles said so.

Then Charles asked the control tower for clearance to taxi out to the take-off runway. You have to take off into the wind as much as you can, and on this occasion that meant taking off over our house, which was rather fun (I felt like dropping a soot bomb or something on the roof!). The lady in the tower held us until a student pilot took off, then it was our turn and we moved off. On the ground, Charles steered the plane with foot pedals but as the engine went on full throttle we belted across the ground and soon I could feel the plane eager to get into the air. Then he drew the joystick back and the nose lifted and we were up, up and away! I realized I'd been holding my breath, but it didn't feel at all funny, flying . . . in an odd way I didn't even feel high up, though I could see the ground falling away beneath us. But it wasn't scary, not like standing on a cliff edge. Even Mum was looking down, more interested than scared, as we went into a gentle turn above the village.

'How clean and pretty everything looks from up here – and the colours all blend together, like a pattern,' she said in wonder. 'And it's not as noisy as I thought it would be.'

'You should try a glider, Mrs Tremayne,' Mike urged. 'No sound but the wind.'

'Thanks, I feel safer with an engine!'

Once we were high enough and flying straight level, Charles began to give us a flying lesson – well, Mum mainly, because she was sitting next to him and could see exactly what he was doing with the controls. He explained how the joystick moving forward or back turned the nose of the plane down or up. Side to side, and the plane turned in the required direction. You had rudder pedals, too, to work with your feet in conjunction with the joystick and a trim tab which adjusts the centre of gravity of the plane or its balance or something (that bit was too technical for me). The engine power was controlled by the throttle.

'Fran, where do you think we are!' Charles asked me suddenly, and I grinned. That was an easy one because I could see below us the golden dome, the mausoleum on top of the Hell Fire Caves.

'We'll do a local tour,' he said, and we did – over to Marlow, following the Thames for a bit; then back, across the Chilterns, to have a look at Aylesbury. Coming back from there, Charles even managed to persuade Mum to have a go at flying the plane, straight and level – well more or less straight and almost level! I think she did very well. By the time we landed, soft as a butterfly on a flower, I could tell she was hooked. Flying had become a beautiful experience in her book, and she thanked Charles profusely. So did I – I was even able to understand a bit why Mike went bananas over it and would certainly take any chance I got to go up again.

But that wouldn't be for some time, not with Charles anyway. To my disappointment, he said he would be away for most of the rest of January and almost all February, in the Pacific (lucky beast) for television location work on the opera *The Pearl Fishers*. However, he promised he'd take us up again when he came back and that was one promise I wouldn't let him forget!

Business did perk up at the Nurseries once Mrs de Lacey's contract switched to us, and Grandad was really pleased – but he was cross because the hospital still wouldn't let him come home and start helping out! He was walking again by mid-January, but very slowly and carefully, with a frame, and because of his age they were not taking any chances. Anyway, Steve had only just started to construct the first of the raised beds for our 'Wheelchair Garden.'

But generally, life was pretty dull and the weather was foul. In the evenings I mainly stayed in, reading, writing or watching telly, or working on the collage that was my school crafts project. But weekends were a bore. Cee went to ballet classes *and* practised a lot at home because she had an exam coming up. Mike was fed up too, because for three weekends running the weather was too bad for flying. So we ended up playing endless games of Scrabble, or fiddling with his old practice engine in the hangars. He even trusted me once with painting one of his precious model aircraft, and I did a good job on it though I say it myself – but the wretched twins got at it while it was drying. Goodnight, one aircraft! How Mike stopped himself from scragging them, I do not know!

One Saturday, we even went to a matinee in Wycombe together – to see *Star Trek 2, The Wrath of Kahn*. We both love science fiction and I found that we both have an ambition to see a flying saucer and meet a person from outer space. Mind you, it wasn't a romantic scene at all, we didn't hold hands in the back row even – though he did lend me his clean hankie and didn't tease me for crying when Mr Spock died!

But the very first fine weekend, Mike's Air Cadet company came over to do some parascending and I had to take a back seat again. Have you ever seen parascending? It's great! Instead of jumping out of a plane and your chute opening as you come down, it's opened on the ground and you're towed up like a kite by a Land Rover. All flying stopped for two hours to let the cadets parascend, and I longed to have a go – but with twenty-eight of them, no chance! The most I got to do was help flatten out the chute when the boys landed. Mike, of course, was in his element – so was his dad and by the end of the afternoon Mr Burnett had more or less decided to buy a chute and harness himself. I hoped he would, because then I would be almost certainly able to have a go sometime! To sweeten them both up, I went home and made some chocolate fudge for them, the kind Andy had always liked.

Andy – he was the cause of some grey February nasties. He'd written me a long letter about what he was doing, which ought to have been nice, only Tamsin's name cropped up every second sentence. Of course, I hadn't expected him not to have any girl friends at all, but it hurt to think of her maybe taking my place so quickly and easily. And to be honest I'd rather been hoping to get a Valentine from him. The trouble is, with a girls' school *Romance* seems so much more important, and I knew all the girls would be showing off their Valentines and boasting like mad. My only chance for one, I'd thought, would have been from Andy and now that wasn't likely to happen, so I'd either be Valentineless or have to cheat by sending one to myself which I didn't want to do. What did it matter, anyway?

But I got two! One was really special – it arrived a day early, and guess who it was from? Charles McLaren! Oh, not a proper Valentine, but it was super nevertheless. He'd sent a photo of himself in the make-up and costume of the young hero of *The Pearl Fishers*, and inside he'd written this letter as from a cannibal chief asking me to become his next bride because he'd just made the last one into a curry. With this was a separate note, saying how he knew from Cee that it was necessary to flourish a Valentine in front of your friends and maybe this one would really give them something to talk about! Wasn't it super of him? I showed it to Cee at once, of course, and she laughed like a drain.

'Keep the envelope with the foreign stamp', she urged, 'and with a bit of luck some of them may even be daft enough to believe it!'

She was OK – her Valentine card had also arrived a day early and David had not only signed it, he'd also put a really pretty little locket inside, and an invitation to go along and cheer him on at a figure-skating competition he'd entered. His parents would take her.

'Perhaps I won't be a ballerina,' she said dreamily. 'I'll perform for a bit, maybe, then teach – that way I can marry and have a family as well. It can't be easy, being a married ballerina.'

I could tell she was drifting down the aisle in her dreams!

As I walked home from school that day, it occurred to me that maybe boys were as bad as girls over Valentines, so I kept on walking down into the village and managed to find a silly Valentine still left in the shop. Then I sneaked over to the airfield that evening and popped it in the Burnett's letter box, addressed to Mike. And I was very glad I had — because in the morning there was one in the post for me — he hadn't signed it but I recognized the writing on the envelope, to say nothing of the smudge of aircraft engine oil! So I had two Valentines to stick on my desk in break. The one from Charles certainly attracted a lot of attention — so much that one of the nuns came over to have a look. She asked me who'd really sent it and I told her it was my friend Charles McLaren who was in Tahiti filming with an opera company. And would you believe it, most of the girls — even the first years who had half believed in the cannibal chieftain — refused to believe the truth, that I really knew a famous opera singer who'd been on television? They ended up more curious about my other Valentine, so I acted mysterious about it, just to drive them crazy.

I hadn't forgotten Paul's rock opera while all these things were going on. It was just that, short of kidnapping one of the performers Mrs de Lacey had lined up for her Festival, I couldn't do much except remind God from time to time in my prayers. And he obviously had the matter in hand, because on Pancake Day (when I was running in the village relay race) Mrs de Lacey, who was starter, asked me to see her afterwards. It was fantastic news! A young harpist and his singer wife who had been booked to do the Whit Sunday evening performance, had taken the booking themselves and forgotten to tell their agent. He meanwhile had arranged a tour for them in Australia and New Zealand. Obviously, a foreign tour with lots of guaranteed performances (and money) was better than a single show, so they'd pulled out of the Festival with heaps of apologies. And most top-flight artistes would have their diaries full months and months ahead, so Mrs de Lacey and her committee were prepared to consider Paul's work.

She wanted to contact him immediately so I told her to try the college, and gave her the phone number of his hostel. That night he rang us to say he would be down on Friday to see her, and on Friday evening he came round looking shattered.

'We're in!' he said. 'And frankly, I'm terrified! Rehearsals with my friends are coming on quite well, but it'll be impossible if we don't find the right soprano. And what about scenery, backcloths?'

'Get Stella to design some, and surely you can find someone to make and paint them,' I said, and grinned. 'Have faith, mate — you've got your impossible tenor and your impossible performance, I don't reckon God will let you down on the soprano.'

'Let *you* down,' he corrected. 'I still don't really believe any of this. I'll wake up tomorrow!'

Anyway, I managed to persuade him to ask Stella to have a go at designing the backcloths. At least, he didn't want much scenery because of the difficulty of setting it up when there was someone else using the stage in the afternoon. And he promised to ask Cee to organize something in the dancing line. Like a fool, I didn't volunteer there and then to do something myself — later I realized that was a mistake, I should have got in at the beginning. But I got distracted by Paul asking if I really did believe in God and Jesus, or if it was just a phase I was going through, or something I believe just because my parents believed, and hadn't thought out for myself.

The last bit was easily answered — it was my decision and Mum and Dad had never tried to push or brainwash me into it. And I didn't reckon it was going to be just a phase, it seemed to be getting better and more important all the time.

Paul shrugged. 'I suppose to me church is all mixed up with the Establishment, with Mum and Dad, things they believe in and I don't; things I believe in that just don't seem to register with them,' he said. I thought he might go on to tell me what the hassle with his parents was, but he just clammed up. He did let slip, though, that his father was a Colonel, and I guessed that was part of the problem. I mean, a dedicated peacemaker having a dad who was a professional soldier must have led to a few arguments!

That night, and the next eight nights, I prayed like mad for a soprano. I should have left it at praying, but I didn't, I couldn't resist trying to fix something up myself. And that got me into trouble right up to my neck!

CHAPTER 8

TROUBLE!

It happened like this. Cee and I went to the convent on Saturday afternoon to see a video of *Chariots of Fire* and as we were walking through the grounds I heard this absolutely fantastic, unaccompanied soprano voice! It was coming from behind the walled garden which is part of the nuns' private territory and strictly out of bounds. I know now that the sensible thing would have been to ask someone to find out who the singer was. Or even more sensibly, I suppose when we'd first wanted a soprano, I could have asked our music teacher, Sister Grace, if she knew of anyone. But that hadn't occurred to me and now I was so excited I had to act at once and blow the rules!

So, ignoring poor Cee's protests that I was mad and they'd kick me out, I climbed over the high stone wall. The singing was coming from inside a potting shed so I burst in and . . .

. . . came face to face with the Mother Superior and a transistor radio! The lovely voice was rapidly switched off and Mother, who'd been planting seeds, looked at me with a mixture of astonishment and annoyance. I wondered dismally how many girls managed to get expelled in their very first term at a new school – although the Mother Superior didn't teach, she had overall authority and I knew I was in big trouble.

'Did you not know that the garden is out of bounds?' she asked me quietly.

I admit that for a moment I considered playing the

ignorant new girl for all I was worth. But that would be lying and would have made things even worse, so I admitted I knew. 'But I had to speak to the singer with the glorious voice – it didn't occur to me it could be a radio – I somehow didn't think of nuns having trannies.'

'I doubt if you thought much at all. It was, in fact, Kiri te Kanawa. Now, how did you get in here?'

'I climbed the wall,' I said, looking hard at my shoes.

Mother raised her eyebrows and I began to hope I might not be for the chop after all. She didn't seem nearly as angry as I'd feared. She was even curious. 'Why did a soprano voice have such a pied piper effect on you, anyway?' she asked.

So I told her about Paul's rock opera, and much more. About his hassle with his parents (whatever it might be), and how he'd gone off Christianity, and the way I believed in his music and how we'd miraculously got the right tenor and somewhere to perform it. I assured her fervently that the music and the words were absolutely fantastic and I was 100 per cent sure God wanted to see it performed because peace was so important.

'But you felt that God needed a helping hand when it came to obtaining a soprano? Or his soprano might get away if you didn't immediately trespass and catch her?'

Her smile took some of the hurt out of her words, but put like that, it did sound pretty stupid. In fact I knew perfectly well that I'd been stupid, acting on impulse, not stopping to think. I remembered Cee, who'd be getting worried stiff, and was suddenly afraid she might climb over too, to find out what had happened to me, then she'd also be in trouble.

So I told Mother I'd a friend waiting, who'd tried to stop me, and could I please let her know what had happened, so she didn't try to come and get me? I mentioned no names, but she probably guessed.

'You may go,' she said. 'I intend to enjoy what remains of my free time before going to discuss your case with your headmistress. Remember – this is not only your school, it is our *home*. We will see you in my study at 4 p.m.'

Thoroughly chastened, I had to go out through the small side gate, through the novices' area, and make my way back to Cee, who was going frantic.

'You go to the film,' I told her. 'I got caught by the MS, of all people, and I'm supposed to brood on my sins till 4 o'clock then see the headmistress and her. And it was only Kiri te Kanawa on a flipping tranny!'

'Oh, Fran!'

Cee was horrified and wanted to stay and commiserate with me, but I really wanted to be alone, so she went to the film, swearing she wouldn't enjoy it one bit and would be thinking of me all the time.

I felt increasingly awful. I knew I'd been silly and done wrong. I didn't dare think of Mum and Dad's reaction when I told them – and I'd have to. And although I now guessed I probably wouldn't be expelled, I was frightened they might take my scholarship away and didn't think Mum and Dad could afford to let me stay at the convent without it. Funny, once I would have been quite happy at the idea of going to a big, co-ed comprehensive in Wycombe, but I'd got rather fond of the convent by then!

At 3.55 I dragged my miserable self to the study, knocked, and was called in to face my doom. The headmistress gave a look which said all too clearly that I had let her down and she was disappointed in me. I flushed, and had to fight really hard to stop myself from crying.

'We do not believe in negative punishments here,' Mother said. 'Every punishment must have a positive side, to help you learn and grow. Sister Anne Grace has suggested something of which I wholly approve.'

'Detentions,' the headmistress said calmly, 'involve study

and essay writing. I regret that, apart from the brief shame of having your name read out at Assembly, you would probably enjoy them. Instead, I shall give you our first Community Service Order.'

'You mean, like the police give young offenders?' I asked, perking up. 'Where you have to do so many hours of voluntary work?'

'Exactly. You will give a large amount of your free time, for the remainder of this term, to help the Community – ours, that is. I have a particular job for you. We like to keep press cuttings of religious and social interest but lately there has been no time. We have a large supply of newspapers which need reading through, and the cuttings extracted, before we give the rest to be recycled.'

Phew – talk about getting off lightly. I had to smile! The headmistress smiled too. 'I know – you'll enjoy that too!' she admitted ruefully.

'We are being lenient,' Mother explained, 'because we both feel your breach of rules was a result of impulsiveness and over-enthusiasm, without any ill intent. You were silly, but I think you now realize that yourself. We are interested in your friend's music and his need for a rather special soprano. You do not deserve assistance, perhaps, but working on the basis that it is for God and peace, not for Fran Tremayne, we think we may be able to help, if the music and words are as good as you say. Please obtain a copy of the score and bring it to school as soon as possible.

'Thanks!' I said fervently. 'I do truly appreciate that you've been kinder to me than I deserve, and I promise I'll try to think before I act in future.'

Then they let me go, and I ran off to give the good news to Cee, who was relieved. She'd honestly thought I'd be given some awful doom like detentions every evening for the next three years, if they didn't actually kick me out. Mind you, when I got home and confessed to Mum and

Dad, I got a far worse telling off than the nuns had given me, plus severe curtailment of privileges – my telly watching cut and my pocket money reduced by half for the rest of the Spring term. Perhaps the headmistress had expected some such reaction when she'd been gentle! Anyway, I didn't feel hard done by – I was only grateful it hadn't been much worse, and I did feel honestly ashamed of myself.

But I was just a bit hopeful, too – so I rang Paul and asked him to let me have a photocopy of the score, especially the soprano bit, as soon as he could.

It arrived three days later. I took it straight to Sister Grace, the music teacher, and at lunchtime she summoned me to the music room. Mother Superior and the headmistress were also there, and one of the prefects, a slender, kind West Indian girl called Mary. I didn't know her well, but she was a real favourite with the younger kids. She was in my good books because she tended to turn a blind eye to minor misdemeanours like running in the corridors, but heaven help a bully if she spotted them in action!

Now Sister Grace tends to suffer from what my mum calls verbal diarrhoea, which means she keeps rabbiting on – even while she's playing! Off she went. 'When I heard it was a "rock opera", I admit I shuddered, but the music is excellent, the words most interesting, and the soprano part is certainly difficult, especially in the range and character it requires. This part – Miss Dove – reminds me very strongly of the concept of the Holy Spirit, the sense of intense purity but with nothing weak in it. It astonishes me that this has been written by someone who claims not to be a Christian . . .'

She didn't really expect us to comment, in fact she didn't allow us time to get a word in edgeways as she talked and played. 'This composer has set a very demanding task for any female singer. Fortunately, I believe God has given Mary the voice to match the role.'

Mary? I'd never heard her sing and it simply hadn't occurred to me she was anything out of the ordinary in any way, apart from being a good prefect. She was a day girl, but commuted from the London area, so she wasn't around for any weekend services and even missed morning Assembly because her train got her in just a bit too late. Then Sister Grace played the most difficult bit, the soft, high part when Miss Dove first comes on. She has to soar above all the chaos and anarchy caused by Mr Hawk as the voice of peace and sanity. Now I can only soar if I shout – even then I can only get up to top G. Mary just took off effortlessly, softly, up the scale, passed top G and warbled around the top C level a few times. I couldn't believe anyone still at school could sing like that – but apparently she'd been trained ever since Sister Grace spotted her talent in the first year. And Sister Grace had herself once been a professional singer, so she knew what she was doing.

But it wasn't just her voice that was so marvellous, it was the whole way she sang – with feeling, emotion, her whole body and face and eyes given over to the music. None of this standing staring straight ahead with hands clasped neatly in front of you. She wasn't consciously acting, she was just pouring all of herself into the words and the music; a bit embarrassed to begin with, she had soon forgotten us and now she *was* Miss Dove, peace in person.

'Wow!' I said softly as the last note died away, then got shell-shocked again as Sister Grace played the next bit – a deep, powerful, beat bit with a jazz sound.

No. Rock opera wasn't really a good enough description – I think Paul had used just about every type of music somehow, though the rock beat was strongest. And the incredible thing was that whatever he wrote, Mary could sing. Like Charles, she was a Genuine Genius.

'She has a wonderful gift,' Sister Grace agreed, 'and one that should be used. Mary is happy to sing the role if your friend Paul approves of her.'

'But I probably won't be good enough,' the silly twit said shyly, and it wasn't false modesty either, she really meant it! She honestly didn't rate her talent very highly. But she loved the music, and was really keen − best of all, living where she did, she could easily get to evening and weekend rehearsals with Paul and his friends, and promised to go along and see him whenever it was convenient for him to audition her. So I rang him that evening, and though he seemed interested, I could tell he wasn't going to risk getting enthusiastic until he'd heard her, not after trying so many student sopranos who couldn't cope. Why should a schoolgirl succeed when they'd failed? But he asked me to get her to come to his rehearsal the next Wednesday evening at the college, and I duly passed the message on.

On Wednesday night after I'd gone to bed he rang up and spoke to Mum. She left his message on my bedside cupboard, for me to read when I got up.

'Paul rang to say Mary is fantastic, and even he's beginning to believe in miracles!'

and underneath, a little note of her own:

'Which goes to prove God works for good in all things, for those who love him, even when they don't deserve it!'

Which, needless to say, didn't mean Paul, but me and my wall climbing! Believe me, I knew it − and my prayers when I got up the next morning included a very fervent thank you.

Mary was starry-eyed at school, thrilled to bits with the music, the words, Paul, his friends, and Charles, who had just come back from Tahiti and was rehearsing with them for the first time. Luckily, her family don't have a television so she didn't recognize him and obviously just thought he was another of Paul's mates – otherwise, she's so shy, she might have been scared to sing with him.

To be honest, I felt a bit envious. It was marvellous that the rock opera (which still hadn't got a proper name) was going ahead, but I did wish I could feel part of it. But even if my voice had been good enough, which I doubt, all the parts had been fixed up now and anyway, rehearsals were up in London. It was easy for Mary to go, and even Cee, because she went with Dave and Charles and stayed overnight at their mum's twice a week if necessary, coming back by train in the morning, straight to school. Even Stella was able to stay involved and was having a great time working on the backcloths – either Paul or one of his stage crew, a Chinese boy called Lee, would pick her up from her Home and take her back afterwards. All of them kept telling me how marvellous it was but not one of them thought to invite me up to see for myself! And I was too miffed that they didn't seem to care to dream of asking (later, I discovered that because I hadn't asked, they'd thought I wasn't interested).

At the same time, Mike was going for his Duke of Edinburgh award, doing hikes and projects and goodness knows what else, so I didn't even see much of him. It was lucky I had my 'punishment' newspaper cuttings to do and odd jobs at the Nurseries, or I would have been really fed up and bored. As it was, I started daydreaming more and more about Charles McLaren, sure that if only *he* would really notice me, everything would work out just right. He'd take me flying, and to rehearsals, and he'd even make certain Paul fitted me into the rock opera somewhere.

Oh, if only he'd notice me as a *girl* instead of just a schoolfriend of Cee's!

Of course, I didn't mention my feelings, because I knew everyone would say it was just a schoolgirl crush (and I suppose, deep down, I knew it probably was, though it certainly did feel like love sometimes. I came over all gooey just thinking about him!). But that didn't stop my heart from going crazy with happiness when, the first Sunday in March, Charles rang to say he was coming down, and would I like to go for a flight with him, Dave and Celia. I was just about to say, 'Yes, *please*,' when – thump, down went my heart again. I couldn't. It had been a busy week at the Nurseries and at school, and I was way behind with my press cuttings. I knew I couldn't do any in the evening, because of going to church, and though the nuns probably wouldn't check up on me, they'd trusted me to do so many hours a week, fitted in when I could, so it was kind of a point of honour.

So I explained to Charles and suggested Mike might like to go instead.

'Fine,' he said. 'You can always come another day.'

I did wish he could have sounded a bit more disappointed and tried to persuade me to come. It rather knocked my romantic dreams on the head that he was just as happy to have Mike in the spare seat, but I cheered myself up by thinking how chuffed Mike would be to get another free flight, and went across to tell him. But he wasn't there. Cee explained that on Sunday morning he had to go to church with his school, so he wasn't likely to be back in time to go flying anyway.

'Just as well,' she said, a bit unkindly, 'he would only show off and want to take the controls, or get Charles to do stunts or something.'

For some unknown reason, perhaps because I knew how disappointed I felt that I couldn't go, I stuck up for Mike.

'He'd be able to get back in time if he knew,' I argued. 'And he'd be dead miserable if he found he'd missed a chance to fly. It doesn't seem fair to go up with only three when there's a fourth seat and he'd absolutely love to go.'

I tried to ring his school. The house matron who answered the phone said the boys had all gone to church but she could catch him when they came in to lunch. That wouldn't do, though, because if they'd got him down for lunch he'd have to stay and he'd never get back to the airfield in time. So I asked her to chop him off the lunch list and said I'd try and catch him as they came out of church. I could just about do it if I cycled in straight away, as fast as I could. In fact, I made it by the skin of my teeth, screeching to a halt just as a horde of boys came out, all well scrubbed and uniformed. Mike was surprised to see me, but when I told him why I'd come, believe me, he was grateful! The housemaster with them gave him permission to run back straight away to school for his bike, and while I waited for him I rang Mum from a public phone booth to ask her to make a sandwich or something for him, in case his own Mum didn't have time – otherwise he'd not have a chance to get anything to eat. He was a bit surprised and taken aback to think I'd bothered and thanked me. Later I heard that all the other boys had teased him about having such a well-trained girlfriend!

Mike isn't the kind who is much good at flattering things or even thank yous. He'd never say it with flowers or anything like that, but he does try. As we cycled breathlessly back, he said that the next time anyone offered him a free flight, he'd see if I could have it instead, to make up for missing this one – which, considering he likes nothing better than being in a plane, was pretty decent.

I saw the four-seater take off as I went to grab some grub

99

myself — it wiggled its wings very slightly and I waved. Disappointment seared through me for a moment, then I shrugged, swallowed my food fast and went up to the convent, to the little spare room overflowing with newspapers.

Well, they say virtue does get rewarded — because guess what I found? Suddenly, sandwiched between some local vicar's 'Thought for the Week' and an article about used cars, was the answer to all my curiosity about Paul — or at least, a good possible explanation of his hassles with his parents. Those friends of his we'd met in London had mentioned a demo — and sure enough, here it was, with banner headlines too!

'Colonel's son arrested as Peace March turns violent.'

There'd been lots of other students involved, of course, but I suppose they'd picked on him because the military connection made a good headline. He was also in a rather awful picture, grappling with another boy while a young policeman, his face torn and bleeding, lay on the pavement behind them.

I admit I was shaken — I just couldn't see Paul as the type who'd beat up a policeman, or anyone else for that matter, especially in the cause of peace! So I read on — not just that article, but later ones, because it came into court, of course.

It sounded a bit sinister. The students had got wind that a certain Ministry of Defence laboratory was being used for germ warfare (it wasn't) and they'd marched on it in protest. I didn't blame them — the idea of germ warfare gives me the shudders — but it sounded like someone had deliberately stirred them up. And though the protest had begun peacefully enough some yobs who had nothing to do with any proper peace organization but were just looking for aggro had joined in and started causing trouble. And people, mainly the police, had ended up getting hurt.

Now I could understand the 'Mob Song' in Paul's rock opera, when Mr Hawk was recruiting some layabouts to bring trouble to a peaceful situation! And I could also understand how Paul's dad must have felt when he saw that article – my dad's no Colonel, but even he would have had pink fits! And maybe he'd exploded before giving Paul a chance to put forward his side of the story.

Because there was another side. I found it in a later report of the court hearings, where Paul was commended for coming to the rescue of that policeman. He'd been arrested, all right, because he was part of a scuffling group, but to begin with he'd been trying to calm things down. Then he saw these yobs attacking the cop and had gone to the man's defence. Carefully, I snipped this cutting out and put it in my pocket – just in case Paul's dad hadn't seen it, I had a vague idea that if I sent it to him it might help to smoothe down the hassle situation. Then I went on dutifully cutting out religious bits until I'd done my promised hours and could go home.

I'd rather hoped Charles would come over to see me – but no such luck. He was still at the airfield when I got home – I saw his car – but he drove away before I could think of a good enough excuse to go over. Oh, well, I told myself firmly – why should he come to see me? He didn't know I was weaving romantic dreams about him!

I did see Mike though. He actually made a point of coming to thank me again. 'Cee said she wouldn't have bothered – she was a bit huffy that you had,' he told me, looking hurt. 'Do I really get on her nerves that much?'

I tried to put it kindly. 'I think she's a bit jealous, really,' I explained, 'because she reckons your parents, especially your dad, give you most of the attention and favours, and are interested in your flying whereas she and her ballet hardly get a look in. She really is keen to do more dancing lessons, but they don't even encourage her, let alone help her. Couldn't your mum run her in just one evening a week? I could babysit, if need be, though heaven knows the twins drive me bananas.'

'Me, too,' Mike grinned. 'But I suppose I could survive them for an evening. Anyway, now Peter's hardly going to Air Cadets any more, I have persuaded Mum and Dad to let me cycle to the bus stop and do the rest by bus. And if Cee did her lessons the same evening as me, I reckon they'd probably let her do that too. I know they wouldn't let her out fairly late in the evening on her own, but with me to protect her it ought to be different. If money's the problem, she could use some of my spending allowance from the trust.'

He obviously just hadn't realized how fed up his sister was feeling, or why, and now he knew, he wasn't spoilt or selfish about it at all, which just goes to show how you can misjudge people. And as we talked a bit more, I could see that Celia had been her own worst enemy in some ways, going on and on about ballet sometimes until everyone was bored rigid, and asking for things like going to White Lodge which she really didn't want.

'She's much better now – now she's got you to listen to her, and has fallen for Dave. Even ballet takes second place to him!' Mike admitted.

Anyway, we ended up with him suggesting that to kind of make things up to Celia, he'd volunteer to babysit with the twins, if I'd help him, anytime she wanted to go to some special ballet thing or even to get her mum to take her to see Dave in one of his skating competitions. And my opinion of Mike went up a bit more – I even found my thoughts straying to him briefly that night, instead of to Charles MacLaren!

'He is a nice boy,' Mum agreed, when I mentioned him to her, 'but you're both such strong characters it was sure to take you quite a while to get to like each other. To begin with, you reminded me of a couple of cats trying to sort out their territories! But I reckon you'll be good friends now!'

And, you know, I rather hoped she was right!

CHAPTER 9

ROMANCE AND CHIVALRY

My conversation with Mike started a mini-revolution at the Burnetts. Actually, our babysitting offer wasn't taken up for a while – but the offer worked wonders. Celia couldn't believe Mike was actually on her side, and I believe it really made her parents think, especially Mr Burnett. It apparently occurred to him for the first time that, as the twins were usually asleep by the time Celia would want to go to her ballet class, there was no earthly reason why *he* shouldn't babysit while Mrs Burnett not only took Celia in but also went to an evening class herself. She'd been wanting to do dressmaking classes for ages! And, though she'd just fallen into the habit of taking it for granted that either she or Celia would have to be available to look after the twins, she began to accept that maybe the men in the family could do the job just as well. What do you know? Women's Lib had come to the Burnett household!

So Celia got her extra ballet lesson – and with it, another friend, a ballet enthusiast of her own age called Jen who lived in Wycombe. By helping Cee I'd spited myself, because although Cee was still my main schoolfriend, at weekends she seemed to be either off with Dave or rehearsing with Paul's mob on the rock opera, or doing ballet with Jen.

Once again, I began to get the feeling of being distinctly left out, and it hurt. Outwardly, everything was just fine – even Grandad had started to be allowed home for weekends, and was due to be discharged for good very soon. I was doing well at school, making myself useful round the house and the Nurseries, and giving Mike a hand at the airfield. But in everything I seemed just to be on the fringes, not doing anything special, not *being* anyone special. It particularly hurt where the rock opera was concerned, because somehow I felt this was *my* miracle and I ought to be involved. After all, I had found Charles McLaren; I had approached Mrs de Lacey. In a roundabout sort of way it was even thanks to me that he'd got Mary to sing his soprano bit. One part of me knew that it was really God putting the whole thing together, but after all, I'd been the one who believed in it right from the word go, and pushed it all the way. And now I wasn't having any part in it, or even much to do with it. At one time people had at least told me how it was getting on, now everyone involved was even too busy to chat to me about it. It wasn't fair!

When I groused about it to Mum, she was sympathetic, but told me I mustn't get possessive about miracles – they were God's way of getting a job done, not something for individuals to gloat about. What mattered was the rock opera being performed and doing its bit to give peace a chance – not that I should get my fair share of any fame and glory going! The trouble was, I felt I could do with a bit of glory, or at least, something I could really get involved with, play an important part in somehow. I suppose I'm just a natural born show-off but I wanted to feel I mattered.

Talking to Grandad when he was home helped a lot. It was easier to share my feelings with him than with Mum. Although he still had a lot of problems to cope with himself, he seemed really to care and understand about mine. Sometimes with Mum I got the impression she was thinking, 'Oh, Fran's just having one of her moods again, she'll grow out of it.' Grandad was different. He didn't ever preach or philosophize or tell me what to do. Often we just talked generally, even about his own youth, which was quite interesting – the Depression as a teenager, then the War as a young father (being a Tremayne he'd gone to sea, not Navy, but Merchant Marine). Yet somehow at the end of a conversation with Grandad, I'd find my own thoughts had altered a bit; and I always felt more cheerful. I think it was through him I got the idea that while I was jealous of Paul and Mary, Stella and Celia, because they were all so involved in the rock opera, they might in fact be getting so nervous they would be envying *me* – the one who didn't have to worry whether anything would go horribly wrong or the audience would hate it when it was finally performed.

Thinking of how petrified Celia had been just before her little ballet school show, I decided she should get a dose of the Fran Tremayne Extra Nice Treatment (especially as I had a guilty feeling that I might have acted a bit growly and cross with her lately). So the day after I had talked with Grandad and had that particular idea, instead of waiting for Cee at my gate as usual, I decided to go over to her bungalow for her. On the way I met Mike cycling to school and he screeched to a halt.

'Well met,' he said. 'Can you face two lots of bad news? And one lot of good?'

I groaned. 'Don't tell me – your mum's taken up your offer of babysitting and you want me to help out.'

'Right first time. This Saturday she is taking Cee up to see Dave do his stuff and Dad has flying pupils, so I have to look after the twins all afternoon. It's enough to frighten anyone.'

I agreed. Two twins to one normal human being was unfair odds. But we just might be able to cope between us. 'What's the other bad news?'

'The End of Term Ball at school,' Maurice told me, making a face. 'I've tried to wriggle out of it, but can't. It's unbelievably old-fashioned. We have to wear suits and the girls wear best dresses. There's ballroom dancing and it's awful if you haven't got your own partner fixed up already. Our school invites your school — the boys stand one end; the girls the other; and teachers and nuns look on or take the floor to drag us in with those stupid dances where each time the music stops you both have to go and get another partner. That type of thing went out with the ark, but it's Tradition and we're stuck with it.'

Actually, I rather liked the idea of waltzing around in a long dress, but I only said, 'Nobody's said anything about it at our school yet.'

'They will,' Mike warned. (And he was right; they gave it out at Assembly that morning.) 'Anyway, do you think you could stand being my partner? It's not so bad, if you have a partner to go with you. You can shuffle round together or skive off and sit talking on the window-sills. I won't have to do the cattle market routine with a whole load of girls who are all probably hoping someone else will ask them, and will hate me because I tread on their toes, then go back and giggle about it with their mates.'

So boys had their problems too! I always thought it was us girls who had the big problem, standing like a row of lettuces praying to be asked to dance or dancing with each other and pretending they didn't care a hoot that no boy seemed to fancy them. (At least one good thing about disco dancing is you don't have to actually dance with somebody.)

'I'm not a brilliant ballroom dancer,' I warned, 'but I think I could get enough coaching from Mum and Dad in time, not to tread on you too often.'

'You'll do — at least you're worth talking to,' Mike assured me, which might have been put better but

107

was still a bit flattering. So I agreed to be his partner and was really very glad he'd asked me. Because it's all very well to dream about gorgeous men like Charles but for a school dance you need a real, live, flesh and blood, available and friendly boy! And as I was getting to like Mike more and more, he would do nicely. Always providing Mum would let me go. But I didn't think the no-solo-dates-yet rule would apply to a formal school dance.

'Now for the good news,' said Mike. 'Dad's got a chute and he's decided we can do parascending at fêtes and shows in the summer to help raise funds for charity. Parachutists and balloonists can cost quite a bit because of the equipment they have to use and they often can't do little fêtes. But we could, because now Dad's got the chute and harness all it'll cost is the petrol for the Land Rover. Dad'll drive, because that's the difficult job; we can use almost anyone as ground crew, and I'll go up. You could, too, if you can persuade your parents to let you — that is, if you'd like to.'

'I'd love to!' I cried. Something exciting happening to me, personally, at last! 'But won't Cee want to do it?'

Mike grinned. 'What, our ballerina? You've got to be kidding. She might sprain her ankle or stub her precious toes! Seriously, though, it's just not her scene.'

But it certainly was mine, and we decided Mum and Dad should be approached carefully, that evening if possible, by Mr and Mrs Burnett, who could reassure them on how very safe it was (after all, eleven-year-old Air Cadets had done it).

Then Cee came along and Mike shot off and we started to walk to school.

'I think he's starting to get keen on you,' Cee said, looking surprised.

I just smiled. Perhaps I wouldn't mind at all if he was!

Mum did not react with instant joy to the idea of me

parascending. Dad was OK and Grandad all for it; even Steve got in a word of support because his kid brother was one of the Air Cadets who'd done it. But Mum could only be persuaded by a demonstration, with both Mike and Mrs Burnett going up. And no way would she go up herself.

'Planes,' she said, 'are OK because you feel you have something solid and reliable round you, but I don't fancy dangling in space underneath a fragile – looking silk umbrella.'

I loved it, though – right from the word go, and it was so easy! Just a few steps to run, then up I went. And unlike parachuting, you don't have to control the chute, so I was just able to float up there, enjoying the scenery. I was really disappointed when the Land Rover turned head to wind and stopped, so I had to drift down to earth again. It wasn't as challenging as sailing, but it was the nearest thing to hovering like a bird that I could imagine and the prospect of doing it on lots of summer Saturdays was glorious! Especially as all the people watching would probably think Mike and I were awfully brave, not knowing it was as safe as houses.

In fact, with the prospect of parascending to look foward to, it was quite easy to endure even baby-sitting for the twins! Mike made two kites which actually flew, and as it was a nice spring day with a good breeze, we went to the far end of the airfield well out of everyone's way and the twins flew the kites happily until the strings got tangled, and the kites vanished into the wild blue yonder as both strings gave up the fight and broke. Then before the twins could build up to a full scale yell, I hurriedly suggested we went over to my back garden, made boats and sailed them on the river. Mum, bless her, had been baking, so first we had cakes and hot chocolate in our kitchen (to the horror of the cats, who took one look at the twins and fled!), then we made very simple boats with bits of wood, string and torn old sheeting. They weren't beautiful but they sailed, and we managed to spend a whole hour sailing them without either Sammy or Sue falling in the river. Then, though I hate to admit it, we made boats for ourselves too and had just as much fun as they did — it was almost a pity when their mum came to claim them!

Mike stayed a bit, talking to me, and he didn't talk solidly about flying either, though he did tell me about the History of Flight project he was doing and I actually found I was getting interested — funny how his enthusiasm for flying had put me off him at first. But then I'd still been thinking of myself as a sailor tragically exiled from the sea!

As he went, he called, 'End of term Friday, hurray! But it's the End of Term Dance on Wednesday, yuk! You won't forget, will you?'

I promised I wouldn't and that evening I had Mum and Dad teaching me the foxtrot, waltz and tango round the kitchen! The quickstep I could just about manage already, muttering slow-slow-quick-quick-slow under my breath.

It was funny, really. Though all the girls at school moaned like mad about how old-fashioned the dance was, I noticed that nearly all of them were going, even though — unlike Mike's teachers — ours didn't insist on it. You had to be at least thirteen to go and the younger kids were even envious of those of us who were going. Celia had cried off because Dave didn't go to Mike's school and you weren't allowed to bring in outside boyfriends. And a handful of other girls had also cried off for some reason, but most girls were going, and all Wednesday the talk was who was going — with whom — and what they were wearing. The boarders had their gear on the premises and I got a preview of some of it — lovely dresses, really expensive-looking. I tended to forget, being a scholarship girl myself, that some of them came from pretty wealthy families. Not that the nun's fees were that high and I knew they took in quite a few girls whose people couldn't afford to pay anything but who'd had family tragedies or something that made a boarding school the best answer for a while at any rate. But there were some rich ones, definitely, and I only hoped Mike wouldn't think I was letting him down when I turned up in the only evening dress I had – the one I wore as attendant to the Peveran Carnival Queen.

I should have known better. For a start, it was a nice dress and I knew I looked quite good in it. And anyway, Mike wasn't the kind of boy to notice what a girl wore – he'd only have noticed if I'd worn it to help him with the gliders or something, in which case he'd have told me not to be daft but to go and put my jeans on! He looked quite elegant in a dark suit; he wore it as if it were a uniform – and the one thing about Air Cadets is that they make you stand up straight so he didn't slouch around like some of the other boys. In fact, he was one of the best-looking of the bunch which chuffed me no end. And his Mum had prompted him to buy me a flower to wear, which really set the scene for a ball from another century. Discos would be OK if they weren't so noisy – but this ball was something else! Yes, it was horribly formal, but in fact the teachers didn't act as regimented as we did. After what was a kind of demonstration first dance, most of them got into little chatting groups and left us to it. I don't know whether I've explained but our nuns are not full habit ones; some of the older ones keep the habit but a lot are 'plain clothes' nuns. They tend to be a realistic, friendly lot. So they chatted easily to Mike's school teachers instead of hovering around chaperoning us.

Some of the sixth formers who had established partners

111

soon began dancing, whirling round on the parquet flooring to the sound of a Strauss waltz. All it needed was a few glittering chandeliers but the lighting, worse luck was modern. There was a glorious semi-spiral staircase which ought to be swept down by incredibly haughty ladies, but the effect was rather spoiled by a nun sitting on the bottom step chatting to the master who took Engineering at Mike's school. There was a proper band and beautiful flowers (though not bought from our Nurseries – I'd missed a chance there). By about the third dance, Mike and I plucked up courage to join the others on the floor – it was a quickstep and we managed quite well. After that we danced most things, and when I worked on Mike and got him to ask a couple of the plainer girls in my form to dance, so they didn't end up feeling wallflowers, I got asked to dance myself by one of his teachers, who hauled me around in a fast and furious tango which I just about managed to survive!

It wasn't a dinner dance but there were nuts and little things on sticks, a free drink which they called Fruit Punch and was at a guess lots of fruit juice and fizzy lemonade plus maybe one very small bottle of white wine. It was nice, though, and there was a lot of real fruit in the bowl, including cocktail cherries which both Mike and I love. When nobody was looking we managed to spear a few on our cocktail sticks! There was a soft drinks 'bar' too, which was soon busy because dancing can be hot work – but we weren't given cokes in cans. Everything was served elegantly in glasses, with ice. I loved it – I think I was born in the wrong age and really belong in some era when life was full of drama and intrigue, gallant gentlemen, coaches and four and lovely mysterious ladies at masked balls.

I was really disappointed when at five minutes to ten they announced we were to take our partners for the Last

Waltz. Of course, the dance had to finish fairly early because we all had school the next morning but I was enjoying it so much I wished it could go on until at least midnight, even if I was beginning to yawn. But we waltzed, and we joined hands for 'Auld Lang Syne', then it was goodbyes all round. The boarders had a couple of coaches waiting and the day girls and boys had parents waiting for them out in the school park – including Mr Burnett's Land Rover.

We were quite subdued and sleepy on the drive home but when we drew up outside our gates Mike insisted on getting out and seeing me to my front door. Seeing as I didn't exactly need his manly protection for a ten yard walk, I wondered with a brief thrill of excitement if it meant he wanted to kiss me goodnight – and it did! Stand by for searing romantic dialogue:

ME: Thanks for taking me, Mike. It was great.
MIKE: Yeah, quite survivable. Thanks for coming.
ME: Er, well I suppose I'd better go in now . . .
MIKE: Mmm . . . and Dad's waiting. I thought he'd drive on in and I'd walk across. OK for parascending on Saturday?
ME: You bet!
        (Moment of Embarrassed Silence)
MIKE: Goodnight then . . .
ME: (Longer moment of Embarrassed Silence)

Then he gave me a quick kiss and I kissed him back and we both more or less fled. But it was *lovely*!

And I walked into the house on Cloud Nine and told

113

Mum not to believe all she read about Teenage Sex; the age of Romance and Chivalry was not dead; and that night I didn't dream about Charles McLaren *once*.

CHAPTER 10

COUNTDOWN

Easter, of course, began the countdown for Whitsun and the weekend after and I finally got to see a rehearsal of Paul's rock opera. It now had a name, simply PeaceRock, and rather clever posters of a stick of rock with the word Peace through the centre. The rehearsal took place in the Manor. Mrs de Lacey had given the cast permission to use her stage and facilities a few times before the performance so they wouldn't have the problem of finding their way around at the last minute. It was almost a full dress rehearsal, even down to the stage lighting and make-up, though the actual rehearsal was in the afternoon. They hadn't quite finished the side flats but they had the backcloth, very simple, suggesting the courtyard where all the action took place. The cleverest bit was a wall — it played a big part because it was used for graffiti. Mr Hawk and some of his recruits sprayed on various slogans to stir up hate, but as Miss Dove began to get through, they were cancelled out. There weren't any big props to be moved around and the thing wasn't divided into acts or anything like that — it was quite short, really, and went straight on through without even an interval which I thought was better. The power and flow would have been lost if people stopped in the middle and were able to go to the bar and eat their choccies and gossip.

Of course, the rehearsal itself didn't flow straight through — there were a lot of pauses while they worked things out and they made chalk marks on the stage to show where people should stand or move to. It was important for things like the dance Cee and Dave did where they had to be moving in the midst of a mob and not collide with anyone. But even with all the interruptions, I could feel that the magic was there. It helped a lot that Paul's friends were a real United Nations, all colours, shapes and sizes – that made the idea of world peace, social peace, a whole lot more real. If they could get on together, why couldn't everyone? Some had brought their friends and families down to watch, but the audience had a habit of joining in so it wasn't always easy to tell who was cast and who wasn't.

Charles was there, but nobody treated him like a 'star' and he didn't act like one, either, which was also nice. In fact, I suppose Mary was the real star and she was really terrific. Paul obviously thought so too!

Nobody took much notice of me. Charles said hello but spent most of the time when he wasn't actually rehearsing talking to a cool blonde who had come down with him. Oh, well – I'd always known deep down he was OK for dreaming about, but for real life I now knew I'd rather have someone like Mike anyway. Stella hadn't come – she was away on holiday with some of the other kids from her Home, and in any case she was coming down to stay with us for the night of the performance.

I didn't feel lonely, though, or mind being left out – not once the music got me. I wasn't even in my world any more but wherever it took me. It had changed a bit from the first songs I'd heard in the van and in our living-room, and now, of course, it was at full power, with all the different instruments and voices. Talk about exciting! In one bit I actually couldn't help curling up in my seat and reaching out for someone, anyone, to hold my hand – and someone caught it and held it tight! Mike! He'd also sneaked in to watch and we both stared entranced,

116

it was that good. I mean, so good he even sat quietly through the bit where Cee and Dave were dancing – it was actually very effective, because they were the Young Lovers, a kind of Romeo and Juliet, dancing together, indifferent to all the arguing and milling about of the mob around them, aware of each other and nothing else, even dancing to a different beat. You got the feeling it was all the others who were out of step, not them. They had what mattered. Afterwards, Mike even admitted that dancing that idea worked better than trying to sing it and said he was really glad Cee was having extra lessons now. He hadn't realized before how clever she was. I haven't got a big brother but it struck me as the kind of comment big brothers only make if they really mean it!

I do wish I could describe it all to you, and believe me I've tried, but when I put it down on paper it is just a pale shadow compared to the real thing. So you'll have to take my word for it that it just got better and better, and the ending was so full of joy and hope that I cried my eyes out, which Mike couldn't understand at all. But he did go round telling everyone how good they were, even Cee and Dave, and he told Paul it was a real winner and ought to go on a record and be shown on television. Paul smiled and thanked him, but he was looking shell-shocked.

'I wrote it,' I heard him say to Mary, 'but it's more than I wrote . . . it says more than I meant to say . . . it's got a life I didn't give it. I just wanted to say something about peace and brotherhood in my music but now it's saying something back.'

'Then listen to it,' Mary answered gently, 'because what it is saying is good and beautiful.'

I had the feeling they'd fallen in love, and hoped they had. Paul needed someone to love him and Mary was just the right sort of person. As for what the music was saying, well, I didn't remind him that I thought God was behind it all. I just took advantage of the fact that he was still stunned and reeling and persuaded him to send two of the complimentary tickets Mrs de Lacey had given him to his parents. I did hope they would come and make peace too – that would be the bonus miracle.

Grandad came home for keeps three days later and we had a big welcome home party for him, with lots of people he knew from the village. The very next day he insisted on Steve showing him the raised gardens for the disabled and went round the nurseries selecting plants to go in them. He also got me to make posters and type out a duplicate letter to go to hospitals and disabled clubs. Mum worried about him at first, but Dad said to let him be because he was far more likely to stay well if he was happy and occupied than if we tried to coop him up and not let him pull his weight. In the evenings he usually stayed in his own flat, saying he didn't want to impose on us, but after a bit we managed to persuade him to visit sometimes and also Mike and I got him involved in our interests. He even came along to watch the first parascending performance we did at a fête and I could tell he was dearly longing to have a go the minute he could convince us he was fit enough.

I sent a photo of me way up in the air to Serena and another one to Andy, back in Peveran. Serena is a lousy letter-writer so I didn't expect any answer from her for ages but Andy always says thank you for anything quickly, so I soon got a letter from him. It was very interesting – Tamsin had vanished from the scene because her dad had been transferred to another branch of the bank he worked for and they'd moved. But Andy mentioned Serena quite a few times. They'd been sailing together. Now I could accept Andy doing things with other girls without any twinge of jealousy, because my friendship with Mike was growing. Anyway, I'd come to accept that 300 miles was a long way away. And I'd rather Andy went out with Serena than anybody else! I think that if both Andy and Mike had been living near me, I probably would still have preferred Andy, but as he was in Cornwall and I was in Bucks., there was no contest. Also, though I still wanted to go back to Cornwall in the summer holidays and hoped someone would ask me to stay with them, what I had believed impossible before Christmas was actually happening − I was settling down.

It showed at school, too. In my first term there, I'd relied on Cee a lot for friendship but now I seemed to be making a lot more real friends, including some of the younger kids. Cee called them my Lame Ducks and I suppose, in a sense, some of them were − the ones who found it difficult to settle, the shy ones. Sometimes, I looked in the mirror and it seemed an older, stronger girl was staring back at me. A girl who still had moods and bad times but could get through them better, come out the other side smiling and a little bit stronger. I'd learned to ask Jesus for help and I knew that mattered a lot. I was even beginning to learn not to get uptight when things went wrong. While it had been fun and uncomplicated being happy, carefree Daffy who didn't think about much except sailing and swimming, I was rather proud of the new me, who was definitely growing up!

Everything, everywhere, was falling into place. We'd got home straightened out, the Nurseries were doing more business and, perhaps most important for the moment, PeaceRock was ready for performance, everyone word- and note-perfect and all the seats sold out. There was only one fly in the ointment − Paul still hadn't heard from his parents as to whether they were coming or not. In fact they hadn't even acknowledged receipt of the tickets, let alone thanked him. I found this out from Mary, who asked if they had written to him care of our Nurseries (which they hadn't). She said he was really hurt — scared, too, of being hurt more so he refused to ring them up to make sure the tickets had in fact arrived, just in case they said they had, but that they simply didn't want to go and see his music performed.

I couldn't believe that any parents, no matter what sort of hassles lay in the past, would be that awful. I was more inclined to think that the letter had got lost and spent a whole day trying to decide what to do about it. I knew what town they lived in, so it would be easy to find their telephone number and give them a ring — if they hadn't got the tickets then perhaps we could put things right, get some duplicates from Mrs de Lacey. And if they'd had them and didn't want to come — well, I could either have a go at them and try to persuade them not to be so rotten, or I could accept it was none of my business and ask them not to tell Paul that I'd rung, because he might not like me poking my nose in.

Eventually, I tried to phone them. But the phone had been disconnected! Of course, that made me really curious. I didn't imagine a Colonel would have his phone cut off for not paying his bill, so maybe something awful had happened? The Other Side got him? I mentioned it to Mike, but he just grinned. 'More likely they've moved. Tell you what, though, as it's Saturday tomorrow, we could try to find out — didn't you say they lived in Rickmansworth? We could get there by bus and train.'

'If they'd moved, they'd have told Paul, surely. Yes, I reckon we ought to go over . . .'

'Maybe he was posted overseas — an emergency, like the Falklands, no time to tell anyone. What kind of a Colonel is he, anyway? I didn't think there were any Army camps near Rickmansworth.'

I had to admit I hadn't a clue but I liked the idea of

trying to track him down, especially as the forecast was for rain on Saturday so we probably wouldn't be doing anything else that was much fun. I didn't have much spare cash for bus and train fares, but reckoned I could just about get enough together and it would be a kind of adventure. Especially if Paul's dad turned out to have Disappeared Under Mysterious Circumstances!

We decided not to mention to our parents exactly what we were doing. They didn't mind us going exploring, or to town in the daytime. We often went to the library or the swimming pool, even to the pictures. Mike thought he might face a bit of opposition because he was supposed to be revising for O-levels but he managed to persuade his mum and dad that if he tried to study too much his brain would seize up. Mine were quite happy for me to go exploring, though I think they wouldn't have been so keen on the idea of me interfering in the lives of Paul and his parents. But I couldn't see that it would do any harm – all we were trying to do was trace them and make sure they'd got the tickets.

We set off early and decided to get a kind of combined bus and train ticket that allowed you to 'explore' a certain area without paying any extra. That way, we could chase Paul's parents beyond Rickmansworth if need be, or if we found them first go, we could go somewhere we wanted instead. Our first job was to go to their old address, though, and that was quite easy. We just asked at Rickmansworth Station where the road was and a bus went quite near it. They were nice houses and sure enough – just as Mike had guessed – Paul's parents' house was empty, with a Sold sign stuck outside it.

'I still can't understand why they didn't tell him,' I muttered, and Mike shrugged.

'Perhaps they did and he lost the new address. I don't suppose he's thought of much apart from his rock opera for weeks. Anyway, our next job is to find out whether the letter's here.'

'And where they've moved to.'

We both knew how to achieve that — go to the Estate Agents whose board was up outside. With luck they'd be open on Saturday mornings. They were a local firm and the man we spoke to was interested and happy to help. It could have been complicated, as the house had actually been sold, but the new buyers were still abroad and the agents were looking after the house in the meantime, so they had the key.

'We shut at noon,' the man said. 'After that, I'll drive you round and we can check if the letter's there.'

'Would you be allowed to give us Colonel and Mrs Kearton's new address, too?' I asked hopefully and he obliged, extracting it from a file. Thank goodness, they hadn't gone too far, just to a place called Bicester, the other side of Aylesbury. I could see Mike doing swift calculations.

'We could just about do it,' he said. 'Train from here to Aylesbury, bus from Aylesbury to Bicester, then back by bus to Aylesbury and Aylesbury to Wycombe and then home with a few seconds to spare before everyone starts to wonder where we've got to.'

'Providing the tickets are there,' I said, but I admit I expected they would be. And they were — lying lonely and forlorn in their envelope on the bare floor of that empty house. I suppose the postman had thought someone would be coming in to collect the mail, or they hadn't made arrangements with the Post Office for it to be re-routed, or something. Anyway, that was half the mystery explained.

We thanked the estate agent profusely and he even ran us to the station. There, we had fifteen minutes to wait for a train, so Mike suggested he got us both a coffee and something to eat while I rang Paul and told him his parents couldn't have replied because they'd never got the tickets. So I took some money and installed myself in the station phone booth, where I got the answer to Part Two of the mystery when I rang Paul's hostel.

A girl answered but when I asked to speak to Paul Kearton she sounded surprised. 'Oh, he moved out four weeks ago, maybe more,' she told me. 'He's living with some mates of his now in a house in Dovehampton Road. I'll get the address for you if you wait a minute . . .'

The twit! He'd never thought to tell us!

'Don't bother — I'm in a phone booth and I'll be seeing him soon anyway,' I said. 'Just tell me — what's happening to any post that turns up for him?'

'Oh, one or the other of us takes it along to college and gives it to him when we see him.'

'Thanks.'

Of course, I could guess what had happened. Paul's parents had probably written to say they were moving, but by then he'd already moved and some helpful soul had put the letter in his pocket to take to Paul and forgotten all about it. So he'd written to the old address. Sherlock Holmes couldn't have improved on the deduction!

Mike laughed when I told him and said that was the trouble with arty types, no common sense and memories like sieves. Charles was the one possible exception and even he had taken ages to get the basic principles of aircraft engines right. However, Mike admitted he couldn't read a music score, and it takes all kinds . . . Anyway, we now knew what to do. Take the tickets to Paul's parents, explain the mix-up to them, and on Monday I'd ask Mary to tell Paul what had happened, give him their new address and get his. The only risk was that they might be out, in which case we'd have to leave the tickets with a note. We couldn't ring first — I'd tried Directory Enquiries and they weren't listed so either they didn't have a phone or they did but it was now ex-directory. Of course, I know we could have simply posted the tickets but that wouldn't have been half so exciting as belting off to Bicester.

Anyway, Mike had got the bit between his teeth and was raring to go, though I was in fact beginning to get almost scared. What would the Keartons be like? What would I say to them? Would they understand how important it was that they came to cheer Paul on, if they and he were ever really going to get on properly together again?

I imagined the Colonel as a fierce, blinkered, Blimpish old man and his wife a cowed little rabbit of a woman. Mike reckoned he was more likely to be dark and dangerous, Something in Military Intelligence. He was nearer right than me, but both of us were wrong really. For a start, the man who looked up from his gardening as we came walking down the road was only about forty-five – I didn't know they made Colonels that young. He was dark, but also thin and clever-looking, quite a lot like Paul – enough for me to recognize immediately who he was. And the calm, relaxed lady who was weeding wasn't a bit rabbity. She looked up smiling as we paused at the gate.

'Are you looking for someone?' she asked, and I said Colonel and Mrs Kearton.

'That's us,' she said. 'Come in.' (Though of course she didn't have a clue who we were.)

Mike took over the explanations before I could begin and perhaps it was best because he told everything in a matter-of-fact way and he also called the Colonel 'Sir' which was either a hang-up from Air Cadets or very clever of him. He explained our movements like a military exercise and I could tell the Colonel was pretty impressed – so was Mrs Kearton, but for a different reason.

'How kind of you to go to so much expense and trouble,' she said, and insisted that we should come in and have some tea.

'I'm afraid we're rather pushed for time – it'll take us a few hours to get back and we don't want our parents to worry,' Mike said.

And I added, 'Thanks very much, but we really only wanted to make sure you had the tickets. You will come, won't you – PeaceRock is tremendously good and it matters a lot to Paul that you should see it.'

'Of course we'll come,' Mrs Kearton said instantly. 'In fact, we were beginning to get anxious that we had not heard from Paul for some while – now, of course, I know why. When he is creating something musical, everything else tends to go out of his head!'

'Which has caused a few arguments in the past,' the Colonel acknowledged. 'But I admit I've never had any doubts about his musical talent, no matter how much we may disagree on other things.'

'Like Peace marches? and demos?' I said on impulse, and he smiled wryly.

'So he's told you about that?'

'I ferreted it out – found some press cuttings. You know they praised him for helping that policeman? It wasn't his fault things turned nasty.'

Mike was baffled because I hadn't spoken to him about any of this – it had seemed too much Paul's secret. I tried to make eye signals that I would give him all the details later and he signalled back that he understood.

'You have been doing your homework,' the Colonel murmured. 'And yes, I was fully aware of the situation.'

'We attended all the court hearings,' Mrs Kearton added.

'And tried not to say "I told you so",' her husband continued, again with that half-smile. 'I have never wanted to knock his ideals, just to get some appreciation of reality behind them. I tried to warn him that subversive elements do infiltrate the best of causes – which he took to be a condemnation of the entire Peace movement, most of which is of course made up of good and responsible people.'

'And neither my son nor my husband are very good at compromise,' Mrs Kearton said ruefully. 'So peace in our household is just about as hard to achieve as world peace.'

'I'm sorry,' I said awkwardly. 'It's really none of our business.'

I gave Mike an apologetic look as well but he didn't seem annoyed, just a bit amused and very interested.

'We've had our fireworks and all said things we regretted later,' the Colonel admitted, 'but I'll write tonight and tell Paul we'll be proud and delighted to attend his performance. And do you think you could get us another two tickets?'

'Not unless there are cancellations,' I said. 'They've all been sold.'

Mrs Kearton looked disappointed. 'That's a pity,' she said. 'Still, I suppose we should be glad they have gone so well. It's just that my sister and her husband are rather well up in the music world; they are the ones who have really encouraged Paul's talent. They moved to Canada a couple of years ago but they are back now and she's the music critic for one of the newspapers, while her husband works for a record company. I know they would have been interested to hear Paul's first major composition.'

She went on to talk a bit about her musical family and how the skills and talents had somehow bypassed her, only to surface at double strength in Paul. But I wasn't really listening – I was looking at Mike; he was looking at me, and we were clearly thinking the same thing. A music critic and a man from a record company – if they liked PeaceRock, the

Whitsun Festival wouldn't be the end, it might only be the beginning!

I spoke first but Mike was only seconds behind me. 'Look, I've got a ticket, but I've already been to a dress rehearsal and so I don't really need to go.'

'Same here, and anyway Mrs de Lacey would probably let us watch through the windows.'

'Oh, but Paul's your friend, we couldn't deprive you . . .'

'We'd explain to Paul, he wouldn't mind, and honestly, we have heard all the music, we'd not mind missing the actual performance.'

Eventually we persuaded them and promised we'd leave our tickets marked with the names of Paul's aunt and her husband, Eric Realgar and Sophie Realgar, with Mrs de Lacey. The Keartons paid for them, of course (which we had to accept because our parents had bought them in the first place).

By now, though, we'd talked so long we'd missed our bus. The Keartons were insistent that we should have tea with them, anyway, and Mr – I mean, Colonel – Kearton said he would drive us home. He insisted it was no bother and it certainly meant a lot less hassle for us so we didn't argue. The Keartons were really interesting to talk to, though Colonel Kearton didn't give much away about his job. And I noticed, when we went out to get into his car, he gave it a quick check over, even looking underneath – for bombs? Perhaps he was in Bomb Disposal?

Not that it mattered – we'd already sorted out the one really important thing, that Paul's parents were only too eager to come and see him. I knew it would make all the difference to his confidence, so now everything was All Systems Go for PeaceRock to burst upon the universe!

CHAPTER 11

FLYING HIGH

For a while, time seemed to stand still. But eventually the day came when we broke for half-term on the Wednesday before Whitsun. Cee went up to stay with Charles, Dave and their parents until they all came down together on Whit Sunday. Rehearsals were happening every day now. Dad had promised to go up to London to fetch Stella on Sunday morning and Mike and I had taken our tickets along to the Manor.

Now we wouldn't be going ourselves we'd had to tell our parents why and that involved explaining about how we'd gone in search of Paul's parents. To my relief, Mum and Dad weren't cross. They said more or less all's well that ends well, but they'd rather I discussed any such ideas with them in future *first*. Cee was a bit miffy because she thought Mike had let the Keartons have his ticket simply because he didn't want to come and see her but I assured her it wasn't like that at all and that it was much more important to have a proper music critic in the audience than to have Mike or me as we couldn't do anything useful for PeaceRock except clap like mad. Mrs de Lacey was also a little uptight until we told her the names of the people who would be having the tickets, then she really changed her tune and told us *of course* we had made the right decision. And she must have got on the phone to the local newspapers because a couple of them carried the story the next day. 'Top Music Critic to attend Première of Rock Opera by Young Composer.' True, they weren't big, front-page stories and they didn't mention that the Top Music Critic was the Young Composer's aunt, but they were publicity!

Paul rang up to say he'd heard from his parents and he wasn't quite sure whether to thank us very much or wring our necks. He hadn't wanted to take advantage of the fact that his aunt was important in the music world. I told him that was fair enough but *he* hadn't taken advantage — but if PeaceRock had something important to say, was it fair that it should only get a chance to say it in Stoke Denman? He ended by saying he saw my logic but he was also scared stiff and wished he could run away and hide in a hole somewhere until it was all over.

I decided he needed something to cheer him up and give him confidence like the Teddy Bears and things that stars keep in their dressing rooms, or the piskies some of them wear on chains under their costumes. So I went shopping with Mum and found a little silvery dove lapel pin. It was in a Christian bookshop and the dove was supposed to be a symbol of the Holy Spirit, but of course it is also the symbol of peace, so I thought it would do just right. I could give it to him when he and Mary and her family came to us for lunch on the day of the performance.

PeaceRock meant work for us at the Nurseries because apart from our usual contract stuff for the Manor, we'd promised to supply (free) any greenery and plants Paul wanted on stage. They could not be taken up until after the afternoon recital had finished, but we got them all ready in a shed beforehand.

Honestly, PeaceRock fever had got into everyone's blood — even quite a few of the nuns were going and Sister Grace must have been playing some of the music in the convent because when the Sister in charge of the gardening came in to get some plants off us, she was whistling one of the theme tunes! Lots of people in the village had part-time jobs at the Manor when there were special functions like the Whitsun Festival so they knew all about it and felt particularly involved because of Cee being in it, and Charles – though he wasn't local – was at least locally connected because he flew from Stoke Denman airfield. So they all cared and were backing it. All the local papers had been told and were sending reporters (it must be nice to be a reporter and get to see things for free) and the local radio had promised to send someone, though we hadn't heard anything from the regional television programme. Of course to Mrs de Lacey it was only one item in a culture-packed weekend, but I think even she had a special, soft spot for it.

And I mean, we were just the people on the fringes. For the ones actually in it – well, they must have lived, breathed and dreamed nothing but PeaceRock, I should think! By Saturday it had got so bad that Mike came over and said, 'Lets's escape it for a bit, shall we? There's a gliding cross country and Mr King needs a spotter and navigator.'

'OK,' I agreed. So we forgot about PeaceRock for best part of the day, while Mike mapread and I kept an eye on the glider and Mrs King drove the car towing the big trailer we'd need to pack the glider in once it landed, to get it back to the airfield. It made a nice change!

We got back late evening, went to bed early and – then it was Sunday. P-Day! (Performance Day for the uninitiated!) I went to early service at the village church with Mike and Mrs Burnett while Mum went up with Dad to fetch Stella. Mum had left most of the dinner ready to put in the oven. Because we were having guests it was none of your common-or-garden Shepherd's Pie but turkey drumsticks, boned and stuffed, roast spuds, carrots and peas (the latter frozen, of course) and she'd already made a very fancy trifle for dessert. I just had to pop things in if she wasn't back in time, lay the table and tidy up a bit (Mum has this thing about my room and will not let me leave it in a nice, homely mess).

Stella, Mum and Dad were first back; then Paul, Mary and her parents and sister. Charles and Dave were having a meal with the Burnetts and the rest of the cast and crew of PeaceRock weren't coming down until later. All the performers were being given tea at the Manor beforehand and supper after the performance, if they weren't too excited to eat.

Paul, Mary and Stella certainly didn't do much justice to our lovely meal. They were all about as relaxed as a volcano about to erupt; not exactly terrified, but a funny mixture of excited and happy and scared out of their minds. Mary's family and my family tried to keep the conversation all calm and normal, but it came back to PeaceRock every few minutes anyway! In the end, Mary's dad, who I think is a lay preacher in his church, said calmly, 'God's in charge of this, kids, so relax. And if you can't relax, then pray!'

I wouldn't have dared say quite that, at least not to Paul, but he smiled ruefully. 'For the first time in a very long while,' he admitted, 'I feel I want to do just that.'

Dad suggested a nice walk in the fresh air might also be good for calming nerves so we did that too, taking turns to push Stella in her chair. It was a really nice spring day, sun shining, birds singing and nobody really taking much notice because, try as they might, they could not forget – at least Paul, Mary and Stella couldn't – that tonight their work was going to have to live or die in front of a big audience, most of whom were real conoisseurs of music. I gave Paul the little dove and he put it in his lapel, a thoughtful expression on his face.

'Symbol of peace and the Holy Spirit,' he said. 'Which did you really have in mind?'

I looked him in the eye. 'Both,' I said firmly. 'You can't have one without the other. Not properly.' Then I grinned because the last thing he'd want at the moment was me or anyone preaching at him.

'Just relax,' I said. 'It is going to be super-fantastic. Instant discovery and fame all round. The message of peace got across like it's never been done before.'

Then I suggested he went off and held Mary's hand because she was sure to be just as nervous as he was, if not more so, and he took me at my word. Grandad, Mum and Dad took charge of Mary's family and showed them around, while I helped Stella unpack in the downstairs room that we'd turned into a bedroom for her for the night. We left Paul and Mary in the kitchen and when I peeped in through the window later they were sitting on one of our long benches, holding hands, heads down, eyes closed, praying! It gave me a good feeling — now I was even more sure than ever that not only would the rock opera be OK, but everything — and I mean everything — would turn out right for Paul too. The lonely, angry days would soon be over!

By the time we took Paul and Mary to the Manor, they were calm — on the surface, anyway. I fancied going backstage and helping to set things up but Mum insisted that, as I didn't know where anything went, I would only get in the way and she carted me unceremoniously back home. I had to have a bath anyway and get spruced up because though Mike and I no longer had tickets, he'd chatted up Mrs de Lacey, who seemed to like him, and she'd offered us both a job selling programmes. We could then stand in the shadows at the back of the hall (which now had tiered seating installed) and watch the performance, which was a perfect solution.

So by 7 p.m. we were in position, offering glossy programmes to all the people in their dinner-jackets and evening gear. In fact, they looked so respectable they began to worry me — surely a rock opera ought to have an audience mainly of young people in jeans and tee-shirts? Perhaps this lot would be too highbrow to like it! It also made me realize what a big, brave risk Mrs de Lacey had taken in getting her committee to back this performance — good old battleaxe!

I hate to think what the performers — especially Mary — felt like as the first notes began and the curtains parted. But perhaps by then they were calmer because there was no going back — it was here and actually *happening!*

And of course none of us need have worried — God doesn't make mistakes and this was his music. I could feel it flowing over and into the audience, from the electric shock of the early conflict to the coming of peace. Nobody just sat listening — it really got inside them. Lots of them were swaying or tapping their feet in time to the music. But I think I was the only one who was at all bothered about what anyone else was doing — the rest were watching the stage, totally intent, part of all that was being sung and danced and done.

Then, at the end there was a horrible moment of silence. I thought the audience didn't like it after all and weren't going to clap. But suddenly, they just exploded! The applause rose in deafening waves and some people even stood up, yelling. Paul and his cast stood helplessly, bewildered and overwhelmed. I think they had been as lost in the music as their audience and just couldn't take in this tremendous reception.

Charles, the only professional, reacted first. He stepped forward and told the audience what a privilege it had been to be part of something so exciting, a brilliant work by a young man with a tremendous future. How it had been more than just a rock opera, though — it had been a gift of God, a work for God, and everyone taking part in it

133

had been drawn together by love and peace, proving the principles of what they sang by the way they had worked as one, though from so many different nationalities, creeds and backgrounds. He said something special about Mary's voice, then he ended with the prayer of St Francis: 'Lord, make me an instrument of thy peace . . .'

The audience were utterly silent, eyes closed and heads bowed. Then the curtains closed completely and the National Anthem rang out. People stood for it but didn't seem to find much voice to sing it with; they were literally breathless, I think! Then, still very quiet, they filed out. We waited, planning to go last because of pushing Stella in her chair and Grandad not being able to walk very quickly yet. But two other couples were also waiting – Paul's Mum and Dad and presumably his aunt and her husband.

'Wait a sec,' I urged, and ran round to grab Paul and Mary, virtually dragging them to the front. Paul just stood for a moment, uncertain, looking at his parents – but I knew from the pride and joy in their eyes that everything was all right. The other couple just discreetly melted away to talk to Mrs de Lacey as Paul led Mary forward.

'Hello, Mum, Dad,' I heard him say softly, 'glad you could come. I want you to meet Mary and – I think we've got quite a bit to talk about . . .'

I didn't need to hear more. I ran to join my family, who were moving out now, and Mike who was waiting for me. I didn't even look back. I didn't need to, because I was no longer the least little bit worried about Paul. Deep down I just knew that the last miracle I wanted had happened.

'Is Mylor anywhere near where you used to live? Chuck me the shammy!'

It was a week later and life was back to normal. I was helping Mike clean up a plane. I threw him the chamois

134

leather he wanted and confirmed that Mylor wasn't far from Peveran – a pretty place, too. I'd sailed there lots of times.

'We've rented a house there this summer. Dave's coming. Do you want to? You'll have to share a room with Cee but she doesn't snore.'

Funny – once, I'd have said yes before he could even finish asking me. Now I wasn't so sure. Oh, I still loved Cornwall, it was my home, the place where I'd grown up – but did I want to go back after all, now, just when I was getting used to a new life? Would it hurt too much to see my old friends, the places I knew so well, maybe to do my favourite things again – just for a couple of weeks, knowing I would then have to return here? How would Andy feel, and Serena, if they were starting the kind of deeper friendship where I would be an interloper? What would Andy think of Mike and vice-versa? Suddenly, I was dithering.

Mike misunderstood the reason, and said reassuringly, 'Dad says there's a gliding club in Perranporth, a flying club in Bodmin and a friend of his who lives near Truro has an airstrip we can use for parascending if we like. And they even fly autogiros out near St Merryn – I've never seen them except in James Bond.'

Of course, he'd probably refuse point-blank to go anywhere there weren't aircraft of some shape and size and as I was now getting quite fond of flying-type things, too, he must have thought I felt the same way! I was glad – I didn't want to try to explain why I felt so mixed up and unsure and maybe make him wish he hadn't asked me. Because I knew it could be fun and I'd be daft to refuse just because I was scared my happiness would get unsettled again.

'Thanks, Mike,' I said with all the enthusiasm I could muster, 'I'd love to come!'

Cee came wandering over and stood watching us but didn't offer to help. She was still suffering from withdrawal symptoms because PeaceRock was over and though there were whispers about someone wanting to take it into the West End, you know how these rumours get around. Anyway, she wouldn't be allowed to dance in it professionally, every night, not at her age. So she was feeling flat and I didn't blame her.

'Mike's asked me to come on holiday with you,' I said. 'It should be great! I can show you all the best bits of Cornwall.'

She managed a feeble smile, then said awkwardly, 'I haven't seen much of you lately, Fran — would you like to come over on Tuesday evening, when Mike's at Air Cadets, and we could just chat? Come straight over after school?'

Well, it wasn't my fault she hadn't seen much of me, but I didn't say so. She needed a best friend (female variety) again, so OK, I'd be it. If it had been me dancing in PeaceRock I bet I would have neglected her a bit, too.

'Sure,' I said. 'It'd be nice.'

'OK . . .' She drifted away, back in memories and dreams again.

'I'm getting a moped next week,' Mike said (tactful reminder that it would be his sixteenth birthday soon). 'You can try it too if you like — here on the runways. We're private land so you can ride it here without a licence, and you don't have to be old enough, either.'

'Me? Oh, Mike, thanks — but are you sure? What if I crash it or something awful?'

'I'll murder you if you do. But you won't. You're not daft and dreamy like some I could mention.'

Mike grinned at me and glanced in the direction of his departing sister. I grinned too. He might not be the world's greatest romantic and he certainly wasn't one for hearts and flowers, but maybe Love is Letting your Girlfriend try your Moped!

The sun was shining and life was good. Unconsciously, I began singing the last bit of PeaceRock:

> 'There will be sunshine tomorrow,
> Laughter and dreams and a peace that will last,
> Born of love, growing strong,
> Growing true . . .'

Mike joined in and we sang happily off-tune, to the music of aircraft engines roaring into take-off:

> 'Just hold my hand
> And we'll stand strong in love
> Till we make that tomorrow
> Today.'

The first book about Fran Tremayne:
Wheelchair Summer
Dorothy Oxley

'I'm Daffy and I'm 13. "Daffy by name, daft by nature," Mum says.

'This is the story of a special summer down at the creek and what happened when we met the kids. We loved sailing and swimming; they were in wheelchairs.

'It was special for me too. It was the summer I nearly split up with Andy. And Podge, my best friend, was transformed into a "young lady". And I became a sort of heroine . . .

'Let me tell you how it all began . . .'

Daffy is the funny, imaginative heroine of *Wheelchair Summer*. She definitely has a mind of her own. And she wants to be a writer.

Daffy is always asking questions – about herself, about other people, and about God too. It is through what happens during this special summer that she begins to find some of the answers.

Killer Dog
Peggy Burns

Joe has two passions in life; swimming
and his dog Sheba — a beautiful Irish
setter. Then one day two policemen call
at his house — and Joe's nightmare
begins.

Sheba is accused of killing sheep. She has
been seen. She will probably have to be
put down.

All that night Joe lay awake. By dawn he
had a plan. He had to save Sheba. He
must get her away — now! They would
make for Kestle Rocks . . .

Secret of the Driftwood Elephant
Peggy Burns

It was Duncan's idea to have the white elephant sale. But when Jilly fell in love with the 'real' elephant, she didn't know its secret – or the trouble it would bring.

The events that followed led Jilly to take her revenge on Colonel Jolly, stumble across some horse thieves, and finally do the bravest thing she had ever done.

It all started on the night of the fire, when Elaine's horse was stolen . . .

This is the story of what happens when Jilly gets herself in a fix, and has a rather frightening adventure. But it's also about an exciting discovery: that God loved her despite what she had done.

Alpha Centauri
Robert Siegel

'Becky felt a breeze, and the fog parted a
few yards in front. The moon brightened
and then she saw him, standing absolutely
motionless as if stamped from bronze.
There, tail falling in a graceful arc, ears
pointed and clustered with curls, chest
bare in the blue light, stood a man with
the body of a horse . . .'

Becky was about to become involved in
an adventure which far exceeded her
wildest expectations. Led into the centre
of the forest she finds she has been
carried back in time to ancient Britain.
She emerges in the middle of a desperate
struggle in which ruthless men, the Rock
Movers, are seeking to exterminate a race
of benevolent centaurs. Becky discovers
only she can save them. . .

Operation Titan
Dilwyn Horvat

'Far out beyond the orbit of the planet Saturn, space stretched endlessly, cold, dark and silent. Into the emptiness the mighty flagship *Conqueror* emerged, its wedge-shaped bulk slicing into the space-time continuum.

'Other craft appeared until finally a total of twelve warships powered in towards the speck that was Titan.'

The Empire rules by fear. It destroys all who oppose it. For the rebels on Titan escape seems impossible. In a desperate race against time, Paul Trentam sets out from Earth on a perilous rescue mission . . .